"Someday  To Do Th

murmured Braden, touching his ice tea glass to hers. "But with wine and a fur rug and you in something like you wore last night."

Enchanted by his mellow voice as much as his words, Kendall's eyes grew dark. "And what will you be wearing?" she breathed.

"Not a thing."

"I'll be a little overdressed, won't I?"

"Not for long."

Her body turned to liquid at the thought. A small moan broke from her lips. "Braden . . . you don't play fair."

"What makes you think I'm playing?"

Dear Reader:

Series and Spin-offs! Connecting characters and intriguing interconnections to make your head whirl.

In Joan Hohl's successful trilogy for Silhouette Desire—*Texas Gold* (7/86), *California Copper* (10/86), *Nevada Silver* (1/87)—Joan created a cast of characters that just wouldn't quit. You figure out how *Lady Ice* (5/87) connects. And in August, "J.B." demanded his own story—*One Tough Hombre*. In *Falcon's Flight*, coming in November, you'll learn *all* about . . .?

Annette Broadrick's *Return to Yesterday* (6/87) introduced Adam St. Clair. This August *Adam's Story* tells about the woman who saves his life—and teaches him a thing or two about love!

The six Branigan brothers appeared in Leslie Davis Guccione's *Bittersweet Harvest* (10/86) and *Still Waters* (5/87). September brings *Something in Common*, where the eldest of the strapping Irishmen finds love in unexpected places.

Midnight Rambler by Linda Barlow is in October—a special Halloween surprise, and totally unconnected to anything.

Keep an eye out for other Silhouette Desire favorites—Diana Palmer, Dixie Browning, Ann Major and Elizabeth Lowell, to name a few. You never know when secondary characters will insist on their own story. . . .

All the best,

Isabel Swift
Senior Editor & Editorial Coordinator
Silhouette Books

HELEN R. MYERS
Partners for Life

Silhouette Desire

Published by Silhouette Books New York

America's Publisher of Contemporary Romance

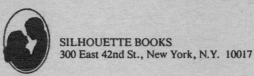

SILHOUETTE BOOKS
300 East 42nd St., New York, N.Y. 10017

Copyright © 1987 by Helen R. Myers

ISBN: 0-373-05370-3

First Silhouette Books printing August 1987

America's Publisher of Contemporary Romance

Printed in the U.S.A.

HELEN R. MYERS

lives on a sixty-five-acre ranch deep in the piney woods of east Texas with her husband, Robert, and a constantly expanding menagerie. She lists her interests as everything that doesn't have to do with a needle and thread. When she and Robert aren't working on the house they've built together, she likes to read, garden and, of course, outfish her husband.

To my husband Robert—for obvious reasons.
And To Amie Yael Inman
who gave me much more than this title.
Many thanks.

One

It was three thirty-five and a Friday afternoon when Braden Manning walked into the downtown Houston police station. The condensed force of heat escaping from the open door hit him like a blast furnace. It could mean only one thing—the central air-conditioning unit had yet to be repaired since its breakdown last night. Tempers would be hot, dispositions satanical and a working environment impossible. To Braden that was as good a reason as any to cut out early.

He shrugged his broad shoulders out of his tan suit jacket and tossed it over his left shoulder, then yanked at the knot of his dark brown tie as he wound his way through the maze of bodies and desks. Even as he released the button of his collar, he could feel the first

drops of sweat slide down his back. Ten minutes, he
decided. All he needed to do was check his desk for
messages, and he was out of there. Despite the heat
wave, things weren't too bad; the cases he was working on could wait, especially considering the schedule
he'd been keeping lately.

"Manning! Can I see you a minute?"

Braden was halfway to his desk when he heard the
smoke-rough voice rise above the rest of the racket. It
stopped him in his tracks. He managed to stifle the
groan of disgust rumbling in his chest, but not the
bitter thoughts. *Damn it, Henry, not today! There's a
cold beer waiting for me at the apartment and an un-
made but comfortable bed. Is that too much to ask
for?* But when he pivoted on his heels, he gave Captain Henry Fielder a tight-lipped smile and began re-
tracing his steps.

"Have a seat," the captain said, as Braden pre-
ceded him into the office. He closed the door quietly.
He was a tall man, only an inch or so shorter than
Braden, with steel-gray hair and sharp hazel eyes.
He'd discarded his jacket also, but his shirt was de-
cidedly marked by sweat, despite the oscillating fan
running full speed on his credenza. Though a man of
few words, he had a talent for imbuing a remarkable
amount of depth into them, so he wasn't surprised
when his polite entreaty earned him a wary look—he
only ignored it.

What now? wondered Braden as he eased his six-
foot-three-inch body into one of the two steel-framed
chairs facing the captain's desk. He flung his jacket

into the other one. He'd long held with the superstition that a good cop could sometimes smell trouble—and it was filling his nostrils fast. It put Braden on edge, so much so that he had to force himself to wait for the captain to speak.

He didn't have to wait long. As soon as the older man sat down behind his desk, he folded his hands passively over a single file and pinned Braden in place with eyes that were as weary as they were wise. Then he let the hammer fall.

"Royce Lockwood made parole yesterday."

Lockwood. Why wasn't Braden surprised to hear that name again? How could he forget him, or the event that provoked one of the few times he'd been forced to draw his gun? He closed his eyes and saw again the courtroom where Royce, who survived his brother during a bungled robbery, was found guilty for his part in the holdup, and faced his two arresting officers vowing revenge. Then, helplessly, he saw the image change to Kendall. She was never far from his thoughts, and she'd been standing beside him that day. His brave, sweet Kendall—who would later leave him—walking out of his life and taking everything good with her.

Braden swallowed against the rawness in his throat, and the ache in his chest. Vaguely he remembered the beer he'd been promising himself and knew now that it was going to have to wait—then it would be Scotch.

"Go on." His voice was a hoarse facsimile of his own mellow baritone.

"I can see that I don't have to." Beneath stark black brows the captain watched Braden's ruggedly handsome face harden. "The word we've gotten from inside Huntsville is that he plans to make good his threat."

Yes, Braden had expected as much. It would be like Royce to feed his anger in prison and not reason it out. He'd always been the hot tempered and impetuous one. It had been his younger brother, Billy, whom Braden could reason with...until that last horrible night.

His silver eyes met his superior's without wavering. "All right. I'll keep my eyes open for him." He didn't want a confrontation with Royce. He even understood some of what he'd gone through losing Billy, but the past had to be kept in its place. All the trials and the hearings were over. One way or the other, Royce had to accept that.

"Just what the hell makes you think you're first on his list?" Henry Fielder rubbed his whisker-stubbed face. Then, to block out the sight of Braden's face turning gray, he pressed his palms against his eyes. "I believe the heat is going to do us all in if the nuts on the street don't get the job done first," he muttered. "Braden, I'm sorry. That was uncalled for. Look," he began again, "I didn't want to say anything until I had something more concrete to go on, but put it together yourself. Lockwood was what, twenty-two when he went into Huntsville?"

"Yeah. He was four years older than Billy."

"That would make him about twenty-six, twenty-seven now. God only knows how his mind's operating. We knew him as a mixed-up kid, and I didn't hear anything from the warden about his turning hardcore. But we both know that when he set his mind to doing something he was like a racehorse wearing blinders. Now I know for a fact that he arrived in Houston yesterday afternoon. Have you seen him? No. Why? Because it's not you he wants . . . yet.''

"Kendall," rasped Braden.

Fielder gave a barely perceptible nod. "From all indications that's what it looks like. But until he violates his parole or attempts something, he has as much a right to be out there as anyone else."

"But why Kendall?" argued Braden. "I pulled the trigger. When Billy panicked and made that stupid attempt— Damn it Henry, I stopped him; she didn't!"

"You think Lockwood's forgotten that? But he also knows that if it weren't for Kendall's gun pointed at him, things might have turned out differently. Maybe he wants to make sure history can't repeat itself."

Braden leaned forward in his chair, and with his elbows resting on his knees, raked his hands through his thick coffee-brown hair. It was a gesture born equally of frustration and suppressed rage. Kendall was out there somewhere, unaware and vulnerable. He couldn't give Lockwood the opportunity of finding her first, no matter what he'd promised her. He just couldn't.

"I have to reach her, Henry."

The older man, with more than twenty-six years of police experience under his belt, had to look away from the haunted expression in Braden's eyes. "You made her a promise," he said heavily.

"Damn it, this is different!" The words exploded from Braden like a cannon. He lunged out of his chair and began to pace across the small office, tempted to put his fist through the sheetrock wall, but struggling for control. He couldn't really afford to lose it—not in front of the only man who really understood and cared. "This is different," he repeated less heatedly.

"I hear you, Braden, but it's been three years. Things could have changed . . . a great deal."

"You don't have to walk on eggs with me, Henry. Besides, we're talking about lives here, not marital status. She'd do the same thing for me if the tables were turned, you know that."

"No, I don't!" Fielder shot back. "I do *not* know that if the situation were reversed and she was the one married that she'd leave her husband to come help you."

Braden covered the space between them in two long strides. He leaned across the captain's desk, his eyes flashing dangerously. "Get it straight, Henry. Maureen is *dead*."

Fielder held up one hand in a sign of peace. "Okay. I deserved that." He sighed and rubbed the back of his neck. "I guess my question is, Why? Why put yourselves through a reunion of this sort? Why take the chance of opening old wounds? Hell, go ahead and tell me that I'm out of line and that I should mind my own business, but I always had a soft spot for you two, and I'd hate to see either one of you in a position to get hurt again. Let me take this another route. I can contact—"

"That's not good enough!" interrupted Braden.

He swung away from Henry's desk and went to the window. His hands braced on either side of the frame, he stared, focusing on nothing but his inner thoughts. Nothing could stop the ache from coming. Kendall married... God, it hurt. And it was possible, even probable. He formed a picture of her in his mind as he'd last seen her, with her golden hair catching the late-afternoon sun. Her deep-green eyes had been rain-fresh because there had been tears in them. Oh, yes, it was probable. A man would have to be blind not to look, and having looked, not want.

But it didn't matter. It couldn't. "I'm not going to let her face him alone, and I'm *not* leaving the job to anyone else," Braden said grimly. "I know you can make it difficult for me, Henry, and I know it's only July and I'm not due for a vacation until next month, but I'm going to ask you to push it up for me, anyway. I want it now. Effective immediately. I'm the one Lockwood should be facing. When he finds her, he'll have to take me on first."

For a long moment Henry Fielder studied his clasped hands. "No matter what?" he murmured.

Braden knew what he was asking, but how could he answer when he didn't know? Three years. People change. Feelings can die, or they can intensify. When it was over—and if he did find out that their positions had reversed—could he be as strong, as principled as she'd been and walk away? His conscience had stopped him from having her before, but he was sure his feelings for her had only grown stronger. He wasn't sure he'd give a damn if she belonged to another man or not. All he could do was try.

"No matter what," he echoed numbly.

For a small eternity the two men eyed each other, one speculating, one praying. Then slowly the captain slid the folder across his desk.

"Officer North is a member of the Corpus Christi police department, and I *am* going to have to call them and advise them of the situation, so you'd better make tracks, mister, because I can only sit on this information so long."

Braden exhaled slowly and reached for the file. "Thanks, Henry."

Two weeks, mused Kendall North as she drove home at the end of her shift. It seemed as though it took forever for vacation time to get here this year. She was really looking forward to the break—not that she had any big plans. It was just nice to know that she wasn't going to have to follow a schedule for a change.

Okay, so she was planning on doing some heavy thinking. Having finally admitted that to herself, she felt better. She also wanted to get started. For the better part of three years she'd been coasting—especially emotionally. Granted, she'd needed to. But now it was time to take stock of things and decide what she was going to do with the rest of her life. Her professional life, that is. As far as her personal life was concerned, she patterned it after an old deserted building, with warning signs plastered across all the entrances: *This property is condemned—no trespassing.* She'd no desire to go through a serious involvement again; she'd just as soon go through major surgery without anesthesia. That's why she accepted only the most casual dates, if she accepted at all. She was too concerned with what others might take as encouragement, and she hated the thought of hurting anyone. A wry smile touched her lips. She had a bad enough time saying no to the simplest things. Braden used to tease her about being such a soft touch. He used to say that she had a dollar for every kid selling candy bars in Texas—even if they were borrowed ones.

Her smile wobbled and died. The last thing she needed right now was to think about Braden. It gave her no comfort to realize that she'd lasted a whole two days this time without doing so. What would really be progress would be to have banished him from her mind forever; maybe then she could get on with her life like a sane person. What would be *terrific* would be to believe that she meant that.

She pulled her Jeep into her dirt driveway, pausing at the mailboxes to collect the mail, and continued on to the house. It was the center one in a semi-circle of three nestled between a series of sand dunes. A small A-frame, she'd purchased it with the inheritance she'd received from her mother. The price had been low because the house had been sorely neglected and in need of numerous repairs, but Kendall had been drawn to it, anyway. A house on the beach was too tempting to resist. She saved a lot of money by doing many of the repairs herself. Though she wasn't exactly a jack-of-all-trades, she did possess an adventurous spirit, and learning by trial and error wasn't an intimidation to her.

She also felt that she'd lucked out by getting wonderful neighbors. Bruno and the Cheeseys fascinated her, and she found them as independent and enterprising as she was.

Bruno, who lived to her left, was a portly German gentleman with an unpronounceable surname. He was a chef for one of the big hotels in the city with twenty-four-hour room service, and his schedule was often the direct opposite of hers, and as a result she often "sat" for his Airedale terrier, Fritz. In exchange—but probably because he thought she needed fattening up—he often made her presents of his culinary delights.

The Cheeseys lived on her right. Naomi and Fred were a couple who had moved to the coast five years before from the Panhandle. Born travelers, they had yet to succumb to the old adage about time slowing all things. Kendall's shoe box, in which she kept all the postcards they'd sent her during previous excursions, would soon need a companion because they were on a train tour of Europe.

Kendall parked her Jeep and hurried into the house. She was a little pressed for time. Adam Rhodes, the district attorney, had asked her to accompany him to a civic fund-raiser. She was often his companion because he was expected to attend so many, and usually

with a date. Kendall was glad to go when she was able.
The situation suited her, and they suited each other.
Each was sensitive to the other's feelings regarding
personal involvement, and respected them. Of the
many friendships she'd made since coming to Corpus
Christi, his was one of the ones she held most dear.
But she knew from experience that Adam didn't take
kindly to being kept waiting. So she dumped the
mail on the kitchen table, grabbed a can of orange
soda from the refrigerator and dashed upstairs to get
ready.

Thirty minutes later she stood before the full-length
mirror on her closet door and grimaced at her reflection. Maybe the green jumpsuit was all wrong—maybe
she should have worn a bra instead of the teddy. The
surplice neckline that was supposed to stay closed
when the belt was cinched didn't, and if the air-
conditioning at this place was set too low, she certainly was going to attract attention. No wonder she
never complained about wearing the same uniform
day in and day out. By the time she championed the
neckline-versus-belt trick she was muttering under her
breath things that would have been more appropriate
for a captain of a sinking ship. The doorbell rang just
as she was slipping on her strappy high-heeled evening sandals. Grabbing her earrings and bag, she raced
to answer. "Don't let me break my neck in these
shoes," she beseeched whatever guardian angel might
be in the vicinity. "And *don't* let the past thirty minutes be an omen of things to come."

* * *

"The next time you see me wearing these shoes, remind me not to," groaned Kendall, massaging her feet several hours later. "I'll be eternally grateful."

"Women," intoned Adam Rhodes. "Why did you wear them in the first place when you knew you'd be on your feet all night?"

"Because I also get tired of having to look up at everyone all the time."

"Of course."

Kendall sat back against the Mercedes' plush seats and smiled to herself. Adam's "of courses" were theatrical gems. She looked at him, and her smile turned whimsical. He was a strange man. Like an iceberg, the majority of his personality was submerged. What he let the world see was only a wry cynic. She didn't pretend to understand him, but she liked him.

"Did you have a good time tonight?" he asked.

"Passable." Sometimes she liked to give a little back. A passing vehicle lit up his face, momentarily exposing his quick grin. In the artificial light his hair was almost as blond as hers. He had strong features and was an attractive man in an aristocratic kind of way. "As usual, I should have eaten more and talked less," she said on a sigh.

"Why do you think I invite you? You keep everyone so busy answering your questions that they don't have time to bother me." He turned off the tape deck that was playing softly. "Judge Farraday was certainly impressed by you. He told me that he was going to submit some of those ideas of yours for youth programs to someone he knows on the city council."

"Really? That's nice."

"Such enthusiasm."

She grimaced. "Adam, we both know that *mentioning* something to *someone* is a far cry from getting a project organized and funded."

"So when are you going to turn in your badge and start doing the work you're so obviously meant for?" He slowed down to make the turn into her driveway.

"As a matter of fact I plan on giving it some serious thought these next two weeks while I'm on vacation, Dr. Freud. Any other questions?"

"That'll do for the moment." He killed the engine, got out and came around to her side of the car. "Why don't you just take those things off and walk barefoot?" he drawled, watching as she slipped into her shoes and got out.

"I'd ruin my hose on the gravel and crushed shells."

"And instead you'll risk getting a sprained ankle. Well then, take my arm. My schedule this week is going to be cramped as it is without hospital visits."

Kendall saw the amusement in his pale blue eyes and squeezed his arm affectionately. "I hope I still know you in another forty years," she said, chuckling. "You're going to be such a delightful ogre. *Ouch!*" She grabbed his arm with both hands as pain stabbed in her foot.

"You see, it pays to show respect, my dear. I have friends in low places. Let me see," he muttered, bending to check her right foot.

"It's only a pebble, I think." She laughed shortly. "Adam, that tickles."

"Gets your mind off the pain, doesn't it? There. It's out."

"Thanks. Now would you mind letting go of my foot? I'm beginning to feel like a flamingo."

"You know, I never realized what small feet you have, North."

"Adam!"

"I suggest you do as the lady asked," a man's voice cautioned from behind them.

Two

———

Kendall and Adam spun around and stared at the man who stood at the base of the back deck stairs several yards away. He was silhouetted against the porch light, and it was impossible to discern more than the fact that he was quite tall and built like a Mack truck. He stood with a deceptive casualness, his hands buried in the pockets of his slacks, but Kendall recognized the danger in that stance just as easily as she'd recognized his voice.

It was Adam, however, who recovered first. He straightened slowly. "What's he? The newest thing in guard dogs?" he murmured with seeming indolence. "I'm impressed, Kendall, but if he bites, I'm warning you—I'll sue."

"It's all right," she managed in a voice barely audible to her own ears. "He's...a friend. My former partner from Houston."

Spotting something unique in her expression, Adam's eyes narrowed with interest. "So, North, another member of your fan club—the numbers and variety of which never cease to amaze me." He nodded his head toward the silent man. "Should we exchange membership cards, or is this where I diplomatically take my leave?"

"Would you mind?"

"Leaving? No. I did have my heart set on a cup of coffee and a few of Bruno's petits fours, but I'll take a rain check." His expression grew almost tender. "You'll be okay? Really?"

She nodded. "Really."

He leaned forward and kissed her brow. "I'll call you in the morning, anyway."

"Thanks for tonight!" she called after him as he got in his car. She listened to the Mercedes roar to life and watched as it drove away. Only then did she turn and approach the man who stood waiting.

How many times had she lain awake in her bed and fantasized this scene? Dozens? Hundreds? For each revision she'd fabricated the wittiest, most clever dialogue; Broadway had nothing to match her.

Well, she didn't feel very clever now. She felt self-conscious, and her heart was pounding so violently against her breastbone that she was positive that the crepe touching her skin must be trembling, too.

"Hello, tiger."

"Hello, Braden."

His nickname for her rolled too easily off his tongue, and her voice came too close to sounding like a caress. In the silence that followed, they wondered about that, and worried.

"You look...good," offered Braden. Then he almost winced at his lack of finesse. Good? She was a knockout standing there with her hair and skin positively glowing in the porch light.

"You look...big." A small embarrassed laugh broke from her lips. "Um, I can't see your face." She wrapped her arms around her waist. Suddenly feeling more like eighteen than twenty-eight, she wished this was a dream and that she could wake herself up.

"You're not missing much," he replied, dismissing himself.

A twinge of despair pulled at her heartstrings. Why had he said that? What had happened to the enormously confident man she'd once known?

"It's been a long time. This is quite a surprise."

"Yeah, I can see that," he muttered. "Sorry if my timing was bad." Hell, what was he apologizing for? He wasn't a bit sorry—except maybe that he hadn't given in to the impulse to punch that guy right in his smart mouth.

"No, it wasn't really. I mean, it doesn't matter." She sensed his skepticism but wasn't about to explain. What she wanted were answers to her own questions. "How did you find me?"

"Henry."

That startled her. Captain Fielder would never have
given him any information without a good reason. She
peered through the darkness, wishing she could see his
face and his eyes more clearly. "Something's wrong,
isn't it?"

"Never could fool you for long, could I?"

"Were you going to try?"

"No. This is serious."

Something was extinguished in Kendall—a small
flame called hope. She drew herself up. Better to know
now than to make a fool of herself later, she told herself briskly.

She dug into her purse and located her keys. "We
can talk inside," she told him.

He moved aside so she could pass him, and as she
did, the scent of citrus and baby powder mingled with
the heavy sea air and coiled his insides into an aching
knot. The tension increased as he followed her up the
stairs. There was no way to miss the gentle sway of her
slender hips, or the way the material of her jumpsuit
softly delineated each delicious curve of her body. He
swallowed with difficulty, his collar and tie suddenly
becoming steel bands that were slowly being tightened by invisible hands.

Kendall fumbled with the lock, then the light switch.
When she succeeded in bathing the kitchen in bright-
ness, she was relieved. This is reality, she reminded
herself. The rest was futile hope and dreams. *Forget
that, and you're really going to make a fool of yourself, North.*

She laid her purse and keys on the counter. "Can I get you a drink? Coffee?"

She turned, and for the first time she could see his face. The weariness and aging in it shocked her. He would only be thirty-seven, she recalled, but he could easily pass for forty. His hard-molded features had craggy lines etched in them now, lines of bitterness as well as fatigue. Still, it was a face she found very dear. How long ago it seemed when she had looked way up into his dancing silvery eyes, seen his mocking, devil-ish smile, and dismissed him as an ex-football star with an ego to match his jersey size.

"I know I should stick with coffee, but a drink sounds better."

"No problem. You can have the drink now and coffee before you—" She stopped abruptly, realizing what she'd been about to say. A rush of color swept up her neck and into her face. "Have a seat," she mum-bled, wishing she could vanish into thin air. She fled to the cabinet where she kept her small liquor supply. "It's Scotch, isn't it?"

"Right. Some things never change." He hadn't meant that to come out almost like a prelude to an in-vitation to go to bed, but that's the way it echoed back to his own ears. With a sigh he pulled out one of the canary-yellow dinette chairs and sat down. He could see that he was making her nervous, and it was the last thing he wanted to do, but he wasn't quite sure how to rectify the matter when all his body wanted to do was gravitate to hers.

She was so pretty. Time hadn't touched her at all—unless it was to enhance that springlike quality she possessed. She still wore her hair in a sleek pageboy just off her shoulders. He remembered her saying once that it was the easiest way for her to manage hair that all but refused to curl. Her skin was still creamy pure. She couldn't tan well, but there was a peachy glow to her complexion that would have made it criminal if she tried. Maybe he'd run across women more artfully perfect, more sophisticated, but he'd stopped paying attention years ago. Who cared when she had something far more . . . vibrant? The words eluded him. He was no poet, but she made him wish that he was.

Kendall carried two drinks to the table, setting the stronger one before him. Taking a sip of her own, she sat down beside him. She didn't really want it; she wasn't much of a drinker, but there was a time when everyone needed a little Dutch courage.

"How's Houston?" she ventured.

"Turning into one big parking lot like the rest of the sunbelt cities."

Her eyes dropped to the heavy tumbler she turned within her restless hands. "Speaking of parking lots, I didn't notice your car outside."

"Nicely done," he murmured, appreciation warming his eyes. "It's parked around the dune on the right. It didn't look like anyone was home next door."

"No, there isn't. Why the secrecy?"

"No secrecy. Caution."

Kendall felt the chill of apprehension envelope her. "All right," she said, pushing away her glass. "Are we going to play twenty questions, or are you going to tell me what's going on?''

She wasn't going to be any easier on him than he'd been on Henry, Braden realized. Part of him was proud, but another part was disappointed. Obviously she didn't share his difficulty in keeping her thoughts focused on her priorities. He suppressed the hurt with a tightening of his abdominal muscles.

"Royce Lockwood is out," he said bluntly. "He's looking for us."

Just like Braden, Kendall had no difficulty associating the name with the incident. The bad ones are never forgotten, and because Braden had been so painfully affected by it, it was etched even deeper in her memory.

They'd responded to a silent alarm at a convenience store one night while on patrol. Royce and Billy Lockwood were just bursting out of the front door when they pulled up. Both Kendall and Braden were stunned when they recognized them. Admittedly, Royce was a familiar face in the county jail, a troublemaker with a number of misdemeanor arrests on his record, but armed robbery meant graduating into felony! The terrible thing was that he had dragged his kid brother Billy into it with him. Braden had tried to take the younger Lockwood under his wing when he'd first gotten into trouble with a street gang, and Billy had seemed to be doing quite well.

Kendall had gotten Royce by sheer luck. He tripped and fell. Billy, younger and faster, might have escaped—if he'd tried. But he saw Royce go down and foolishly tried to save him.

"Let him go!" he yelled, frantically swinging his gun from Braden to Kendall, who was busily hand-cuffing Royce.

"Billy, you know we can't." Braden said, trying to explain.

But Billy, in his state, wasn't listening. He swung the gun back toward Kendall and fired. Maybe he'd meant to miss, or maybe the shot had been accidental. Billy was inexperienced with guns, and there was no telling what he'd meant to do, not even when he swung it back to Braden and it fired again.

At the inquiry, and later the trial, opinion concurred with Braden's actions: he'd had no choice but to defend himself and his partner. But that hadn't meant a thing to Royce.

"I'll get you," he whispered, just before they took him away, his eyes filled with hatred. "I'll get out one day, and when I do, I'll find you. That's my promise to Billy."

Threats weren't exactly uncommon in their profession, but there was something twice as unsettling about Royce's. Maybe it was the dead certainty with which he made his promise, or the irrational anger. Kendall didn't know. Anyway, despite her attempts to put it behind her, she didn't always succeed. She doubted Braden did, either.

"It's strange how sometimes you think you've conquered all your ghosts, learned to tuck the bad moments securely in the back of your mind," she murmured vaguely. "And then you'll be in the car, and a call comes in—the same kind of call, the same kind of voice..." She shook her head. Her eyes refocused, and she gave him a sad smile. "Did you ever make peace with yourself over Billy?" she asked.

"Yeah. Eventually."

"I'm glad."

And so this is why he'd come. Thank goodness she hadn't done anything impulsive like running into his arms, she thought in relief. His motivation had been friendship and concern for an old partner. How embarrassing it would have been if she'd given in to her first impulses.

"Well," she said, drawing in a long breath. "That's quite an announcement. It was good of you to come all this way to warn me."

"Goodness had nothing to do with it. We were partners."

"Yes, but—you could always have phoned."

"Would you?" he demanded.

Kendall's gaze dropped from the challenge she saw in his. They fell to his hands, wrapped tightly around his glass. Like the rest of him, they were large, tanned and capable. The dusting of dark hairs on the back reminded her of the thicker mat of hair covering his chest, and the way her senses had reacted to seeing him without his shirt on. The hands of a receiver on the body of a linebacker, was the way she'd once heard him described. All she knew was that every inch of him was perfect... and sexy.

"Kendall?"

Startled, she snapped her head up. "Yes?"

"Would you have just phoned?"

It wasn't fair of him to remind her of how close they'd been. Maybe he was only referring to their friendship, but even so it was wrong, and dangerous. She could hardly believe herself a second later when she found herself shaking her head. "No, I suppose not.

"So, what are you going to do? I mean, I'm here in Corpus, but Royce's turf is Houston, which logically puts you in the immediate scope of danger. Did Captain Fielder put you on leave and tell you to lie low while they hope he does something foolish and breaks parole?"

"I've taken my vacation."

She nodded approvingly. "That's probably the best."

"Kendall . . ." Braden closed his eyes, feeling dread at merely saying the words. "Lockwood wants you first."

It took a moment for the words to register. All her thoughts, her concern had been centered on Braden. *She* was the first target? "Why?" she asked, honestly confused. "Scratch that," she said with a frown, not at all liking the way it had sounded. "I mean, I'm relieved and grateful to know that for the moment you don't have to keep looking over your shoulder at every sound of footsteps, but I don't understand his logic."

Relieved for him . . . grateful. Braden downed the rest of his drink and rose. The bottle was still on the counter, and he helped himself to another drink, this time not bothering to add the ice. Was he ever going to get used to the way she always put herself second to another person's needs, another's danger? He'd found the characteristic endearing, sometimes amusing when it involved something less serious. But this was serious, and it filled him with terror as he thought of the chances she might be willing to take.

"I'm not about to credit Lockwood with the ability to use logic," he replied tightly. "But for want of a better word, his *logic* seems to be to remove the person who'd stopped him from helping Billy—you. Henry finds it plausible. He says that Lockwood hit town yesterday, and this morning somebody reported having briefly seen him in your old neighborhood."

"I see." That explained Braden's anger. She could feel it emanating like heat from his body. He felt responsible for this turn of events. As he sat back down beside her, she gave him an encouraging smile. "Hey, it's all right. Look, first thing tomorrow morning I'll call headquarters. Within an hour I'll probably have so much backup I'll be ready to start pulling my hair out."

"No, you won't, because I'm going to be your backup."

"Excuse me?"

"I'm staying, Kendall."

"In Corpus Christi?"

"Warm. In this house."

This time it was Kendall's turn to get up. She paced across the length of the kitchen and back again. For the first time this evening she felt a twinge of panic.

She could cope with Royce if she had to. She could even understand him in a crazy kind of way. But Braden, here?

She turned to face him, her expression set. "I'm sorry, but that's impossible."

"Why?"

"Because you *can't*, that's all."

"Not good enough," he said dismissively. "You're obviously not married, otherwise you wouldn't have been out with that guy just now, and I'd assumed you were living alone; but if there's a roommate—"

"I don't have a roommate."

"Then I don't see the problem." He glanced around. "I realize this is a small place. If you haven't got a spare bed, I guess I can survive a few nights on the couch."

The image of that had her turning away abruptly. She went to the sink and clutched the edge of the countertop. Staring out the window past her own reflection, she watched the moon lose its golden color as it rose higher in the ink-black sky. "Braden, I don't need this," she began quietly. "This is my home now. I've made a new life for myself. Houston is the past, and I want to keep as much of it there as possible."

Braden felt as though he'd just taken a direct blow to the stomach. "I understand." He rose and brought her his glass. "Here. Take a sip of this," he said gruffly. "I can appreciate what it cost you to say that." He watched as she unconsciously placed her lips over the exact spot where his own had been moments before. When she handed it back to him, he moved a step away, as much for her peace of mind as his own.

"I understand," he repeated. "But there's something you've forgotten. This thing with Lockwood started out as our joint problem, and it'll end that way. I don't walk out on my partners. Ever."

"You're out of your jurisdiction," she reminded him.

"Henry's making some calls. It'll be taken care of."

In other words, the matter was out of her hands. Fighting Braden was usually a losing proposition all by itself; if Captain Fielder had signed on as an ally, the battle would be over before it had even begun.

"Manning..." The glare she gave him spoke volumes. "What am I going to do with you?"

Talk about loaded questions, he moaned silently. He took a strained breath. Easy does it, pal. You've gotten this far; don't blow it now.

"Well, North, you could relieve my mind and tell me you've got that extra bed. In all honesty, I hate sofas; they're never long enough."

Helplessly Kendall's lips curved. "Yes, I have a spare bed."

"No problem, then. I'll just go get my bag, and then you can give me the grand tour."

Kendall watched as the screen door bounced closed behind him. What have I let myself in for? she wondered. She shook her head and retrieved their glasses, placing them in the sink. The last thing either one of them needed now was more alcohol.

It would be a lie to say that she wasn't glad to see him. The question was, Could she handle it? That line he'd given her about never walking out on a partner was all well and good, but they had extended their relationship beyond parameters acceptable in either their professional or personal lives. Fine, she'd walked away before things had gone too far, but this was her home. Where was she supposed to run if temptation presented itself again? And she knew it could. The way she'd caught him looking at her and the way she'd been looking at him made that obvious.

Get a hold of yourself, she directed. They were just going to have to make the best of this situation and try to resolve it as soon as possible. She went to the living room and turned on a few lamps. From outside came the sound of a car door slamming. He'd be back in a minute. Admit it, she told herself, you'd rather face this with him than without him, wouldn't you?

When Braden returned, he found her making coffee. She didn't turn to give him so much as a look, which in turn made him pause, trying to gauge her mood.

"You didn't move your car," she murmured, adjusting the flame under the pot.

"It's fine where it is tonight."

"Do you think he could have located me this quickly?"

"These days? It's possible. Only the very guilty and the very rich have successfully learned to disappear when they want to."

She turned. "What's going to happen when he realizes you're down here? He's not stupid; he'll smell a trap, especially if headquarters insists on giving me additional backup. All he has to do is back off and wait you out."

"He's not stupid," Braden agreed, "but he's also not the most patient character we've ever met, is he? And he wants revenge. I'm counting on that being the big motivator. I'm also counting on being able to talk your people out of any other obvious backup. What with the tourists and conventions pouring into town, this is your busy season, so maybe that'll be fairly easy."

"That still leaves you," she challenged.

"What makes you think he'll automatically know we're onto him? He didn't exactly put an ad in the paper. Sure, he mouthed off in prison, but they all do. He'll probably see us together, decide we're having an affair and think it's his lucky day, that we'll be too preoccupied with each other to ever see him coming."

"That's not funny, Braden!" She rubbed the spot between her tawny brows that was beginning to throb and took a calming breath. "I'm not exactly having an easy time with this as it is, and I don't appreciate any suggestions—"

"I'm not suggesting anything," he interrupted, his voice as tense as hers. "This isn't exactly a picnic for me, either. You asked me how I thought this was going to go down; I told you." His expression softened, a change that did dangerous things to her resolve. "All you have to do is remember that I'm on your side, okay?''

Great. Now if only she knew what side that was. The coffee began to perk behind her. She turned to readjust the flame. ''This is going to take a few minutes. If you'd like to take your bag up—''

''I don't get the grand tour?'' he teased.

She could just picture that, taking him upstairs, showing him her room—*and this is where I sleep, dreaming of you*. She shook her head, as if to clear it. ''There's not much to warrant a tour, grand or otherwise. As you can see, this is the kitchen, and that's the living room. Upstairs there's a bathroom and two bedrooms. You can have the one next to the bathroom.''

Braden crossed the room and set down his bag by the doorway leading to the living room. As he slipped out of his jacket, he made a more thorough inspection of her home. The living room was paneled in honey-stained cedar. Her furniture was almost as old as his, and there wasn't much of it—obviously she wasn't into clutter—but what there was seemed solid. The kitchen was papered in a warm beige-and-gold flowery print. When the morning sun came through the dinette window, it would make the room a cozy place to linger over coffee and conversation. He laid his jacket over the back of his chair and slipped out of his shoulder holster's harness.

''I like it,'' he told her. ''It looks homey.''

''Thanks.'' She watched him hook the holster onto the chair beneath his jacket. He carried a nine millimeter these days, and something about it and his appearance triggered a memory. "When did you make detective?" she ventured.

He gave her another admiring look. "Six months after you left," he replied, straddling the chair backward.

"Detective Braden Manning," she mused softly.

"Detective *Sergeant*," he corrected with a twinkle in his eye.

"Really? That's wonderful!"

He stared at what was her first spontaneous smile of the evening. It kindled something long dead inside him.

"I'm so proud of you," she continued. "You wanted that more than anything."

Not quite, he corrected silently. There was one thing that would have surpassed it. Slowly he pulled at his tie and released the top two buttons of his shirt. "You'll never guess who my partner is," he said, rolling up his shirtsleeves. "Remember Parnecki?"

Suddenly he found himself talking, like he hadn't in months, years, sharing the memories, the laughs, the sorrows. He confessed how stakeouts were every bit as monotonous as reported; how he still tried to pass on the chore of typing reports to his partner if he could get away with it; how going to court to testify on one of his arrests still made him edgy. Kendall listened intently, asking questions that underlined her interest and encouraged him to share more. He hadn't realized how much he'd missed it, hungered for it, having someone to talk to who really cared. She'd always been a good listener; it was one of the many things that made her so well liked.

Before he knew it, she was setting a steaming mug of coffee on the table behind him. He made a face. "Why didn't you tell me to put a lid on it?"

"Why?" she asked, taking her seat again. "I enjoyed listening. I learned that you're as good in that field as I thought you'd be, and that you like it."

"I like it."

"Good. Now go on. You've only skimmed the surface."

"No, no. That's enough for now."

She traced the rim of her mug with her index finger, repressing a smile. He'd changed. When she'd first met him, he'd been more than willing to talk, "show her the ropes" as he put it. She'd always thought it was more like trying to impress her. He'd been a little macho, and anxious to protect. They'd had some interesting moments as she enlightened him to her interpretation of job equality.

"All right, then, let's get back to Royce," she said. "What do we do next?"

Braden shrugged. "Wait. Tomorrow we'll check in with your people, and then we'll just have to see what his first move is."

"And you're sure he'll come?"

"He'll come."

The certainty with which he answered caused a chill to race down her spine, and she shifted closer to the warmth of her coffee. The movement accentuated the delicate line of her collarbone and drew Braden's gaze, but she didn't notice. Her thoughts were on Royce Lockwood. She bore him no ill will, and she certainly didn't want him to die. If only they could talk to him, reason with him....

"What are you thinking?" Braden asked, lifting his gaze to study her troubled eyes.

She wasn't sure he'd like it if she told him, so she detoured to something else. "Let's just say this isn't the way I planned to spend my vacation."

"Sorry," he muttered, lying through his teeth. "Big plans?" It did no good to tell himself that it was none of his business. He wanted to know. If there were someone else, like that guy in the Mercedes for instance.

"No. No plans at all. Just relaxing." She caught his quick look and misread it. "Yeah, I know. It doesn't sound like me, right?" He'd once told her she didn't know how to relax. She was always into something, from night classes to volunteer work to athletics. In fact the first time they met was at a police softball game. She caught his frown and gave an amused chuckle. "Don't worry. I'm not sick or anything. I just thought I needed a break."

She probably did, but he doubted she'd last three days. "I thought you might be going home—I mean back to St. Louis for a visit," he said, cautious of her sensitivity about the subject. To his amazement her expression brightened.

"You don't know, do you? Of course not, most of it happened after I left Houston. Well, there's been a thaw in the North family relations."

Braden knew about her unhappy childhood, how, after her mother died, her father had been so devastated that he'd been unable to feel anything for the child she'd left behind. How, despite her older brother's efforts to intercede, she'd spent the majority of her childhood in boarding schools where she learned her greatest lessons about neglect and the need for compassion.

"When I left the department, I was feeling . . . well, you know. I thought it might be as good a time as any for my annual visit home. At the very least I wanted to spend a little time with my brother, James. He's always been pretty decent, even if he does let my father run over him like a steamroller.

"Anyway, when I arrived, it was to the news that my father had just suffered a stroke the day before, and he wasn't expected to pull through. I went to the hospital, and I just stood there looking at him. All I could think was that I couldn't let him die without having given me my chance to know him yet. I wouldn't let him cheat me out of that. So I climbed on the bed beside him, took his hand in mine and started to talk to him—I can't even remember about what. But I talked until I was hoarse and the night nurse threw me out. The next day I was back, and I started all over again. I brought books from his library to read to him, and on the fourth day I was stumbling over a passage by Rousseau in French. My French was always atrocious. The passage was something to the effect of: 'Patience is bitter, but its fruit is sweet.' He opened his eyes and said in his inimitable fashion, 'Kendall, if that's the best those teachers of yours could do, I'd have done better to have kept you at home and saved my money.' '' She shook her head, remembering. "I started to laugh and cry and told him maybe he should have."

There were tears in her eyes now, and with feelings too strong to repress, Braden reached across the table to cover her small hand with his own. "I'm glad. God, I'm so glad for you," he whispered.

"Thanks." She blinked back her tears, a little embarrassed. "I don't think we'll ever win an award for family of the year, but things are better." She cleared her throat. "Okay, enough of the violin stories. It's your turn. Why don't you tell me about the old gang? Has Sergeant Mullins retired like he was always threatening to do whenever administration called for a petty change in reporting procedures? And what about you? Come on, you've hardly told me a thing."

Braden lifted her ringless left hand and stared at it for endless seconds. "Well, the old gang is pretty much the same," he began. "Mullins is still threatening. As for me, that's easy." He lifted his gaze to lock with hers. "I still miss you like hell."

Shock, pleasure, dismay... they shot through Kendall like a bolt of lightening leaving her hot and shivering simultaneously. In sheer panic she recoiled, pulling her hand free from his and leaping to her feet, almost knocking over her chair in the process. She took several steps before realizing that as she'd previously feared, there was no place to run. With a small moan, she leaned her forehead against the coolness of the refrigerator door.

"Kendall..." Braden came up behind her, boxing her in with his arms. "Honey..."

"Don't start, please!"

Behind her, his face contorted from a pain too long repressed. "Oh, God, don't you think I've tried?" He lowered his head and drew in the fresh clean scent of her hair. "I swear I have. I've done everything I could to convince myself that what's between us doesn't exist, but it's no good."

She began to protest, until his warm breath brushed her ear. Then he actually touched her there, and she bit her lip against the sensations caused by that fleeting sensual assault.

"I eat...I sleep...I work..." he said in a tormented whisper. "I go through all the motions like some damned programmed machine, but I never forget. Not you, or what it was like to kiss you." His hands moved to her shoulders, massaged her lightly through the crepe, then stroked down her arms. "I can't forget." He slid his arms around her waist and urged her to lean back against his hard body. Slowly his thumbs stroked her in sensual circles that burned through her clothing and robbed her of clear thought.

Kendall moaned softly as her body began to betray her, responding to his touch as though it had always relied on it for sustenance. She could feel her blood begin to race, flowing into her breasts and making them swell and ache.

"Braden, this has got to stop," she pleaded. "Don't—please don't touch me anymore."

"I've got to. The memory of what it was like is driving me crazy."

She felt his heart pound against her back, felt the tension in him, and it was almost as seductive as his words. She wasn't even aware that he had turned her, until her face was framed within his big hands.

"I have this one perfect memory of when you let me kiss you," he said in a rough whisper. He traced her lower lip with his thumb. It trembled beneath the caress, and helplessly her lips parted. As he watched, Braden's eyes dilated. "Yes... like that." He lowered his head. "You let me inside. Let me again...let me."

He covered her mouth with his, drinking her breath as though he were starving. He groaned and raked his fingers deeper into her hair, holding her fast. A terrible hunger clawed at him. He wanted to get closer, needed to. She was so warm, so soft, so damned delicious.

Kendall felt herself growing weak, as if her bones were melting. Behind her closed lids lights flashed and spun madly. Desperately she sought for a hold with her fingers and curled them into the fabric of his shirt.

It was like the last time, their first time, only wilder, sweeter. It was a dream come to life, a wish gone out of control...and it was so very wrong.

Braden's need was spreading like a runaway fire, threatening to consume him. Every inch of her sweet body was pressed against him, but it wasn't enough. He'd been denied her too long. His possession altered. Slipping his strong arms around her, he molded her even closer.

"Braden—no," she moaned. "We have to stop."

"Oh, sweet, remember? *Remember*?"

All too well, she realized. Too well to give in to this, no matter how much she wanted it. Tears flooded her eyes. With her last ounce of willpower she wrenched her head away from his seeking mouth, already despising herself for what she was about to say.

"I remember," she sobbed. "Obviously better than you do. What about Maureen, Braden? When do you remember your *wife*?"

Three

Braden froze. The utter bleakness in his eyes was more than Kendall could bear, and with no small shame, she averted her gaze. A moment later she was free, and he was walking away.

She slumped back against the refrigerator and closed her eyes. What had she done? How could she? If only she could make him realize that it had been the only thing she could think of that would stop him, to remind him how wrong they would be to give in to their desire.

Miserable, she followed him into the living room. He stood there, with his back to her, his hands clenched at his sides. The silence was unbearable, but she was wary of breaking it. She'd never seen him quite like this before, not even when she'd told him she was leaving Houston and the force.

His head rolled back on a ragged sigh. Kendall waited. Maybe she knew him better than she wanted to admit. He was a man of deep emotions that were rigidly controlled from years of training and self-discipline. A few moments ago he'd almost lost that control. She had to allow him the time to regain it.

"I'm sorry," she said at last. "That was an awful thing to throw at you."

"Apologies are unnecessary, tiger. All's fair when you're fighting for survival."

"Stop it!" She hated the self-recrimination and defeat she heard in his voice. "I was wrong, okay? I could have..."

He turned and she gestured feebly.

"You could have what?" He lifted his brow in subtle mockery. "Look at us. Sure, you've got the training to defend yourself, but I'm a foot taller and easily a hundred pounds heavier. And I know all the moves to counter yours," he added with grim confidence. He slid his hands into his pants pockets, curling them into fists. "There's not much you could really have done if I lost my head completely."

Kendall rejected the thought. She had to. "Don't say that. You wouldn't have—*you're not like that*."

Braden's eyes burned with unfulfilled hunger as he raked them over her. "I want you," he said roughly. "So much that I think it's slowly killing me." He drew a ragged breath. "Hell, yes...I could be like that."

He watched her expression as she weighed his words, watched the way shock melted into tenderness, and felt desire sear through him like a blowtorch making small work of a piece of tin. He managed to hold himself in rigid check, but when she made a movement to come toward him, he had no choice but to warn her off, for both their sakes.

"Don't! For God's sake...do you think I want your pity? Look, there's something you need to know, something I should have told you the moment I arrived." He swallowed down the bitter taste that formed in his mouth and forced himself to meet her confused look. "Maureen is dead."

Dead. Despite the fact that Kendall had been aware of Maureen's illness, knew that there was no cure, she still felt the shock the word carried. It was because Maureen had been young, and with the young there's always part of a person's mind that believes that something in that youth will create a miracle that will cheat death. Kendall had prayed for that miracle for Maureen.

Kendall and Braden were still partners when he first learned his wife was diagnosed as being terminally ill. It was the ultimate blow to a marriage that seemed to have begun to disintegrate almost from its beginning. Maureen and Braden had been college sweethearts, and Maureen had been excited at the prospect of marrying Braden and sharing the celebrity of his promising pro-football career. But Braden made choices that killed those dreams: first with volunteering to join the marines and going to Vietnam, and then becoming a cop.

As Braden's partner and friend, it was difficult for Kendall to stand by and watch him struggle to make his marriage work, to see him try to hide his anger and worry when he and Maureen had had a particularly bad fight. Then, as it became more and more obvious that the feelings between Braden and herself were intensifying, Kendall felt as if she were being split in two. She opted to leave; one shattering moment of passion gave her no choice.

Braden had begged her not to go, but she'd left, anyway. As much as she loved him and ached for what he was going through—and what he would go through—she knew what would happen if she stayed, and how wrong it would be.

Kendall looked across the room to where Braden stood studying a painting of the ocean on a peaceful night. She could imagine what he was thinking, perhaps wondering when the last time had been when his soul had felt so untroubled. The urge to go to him was great, but then a nagging doubt began to filter into her thoughts.

Braden turned his head suddenly, and his eyes narrowed. Why didn't she say something? If only he had the right to take her into his arms. He would love her, so slowly, so thoroughly, that they would both forget the past. He'd never meant to drag her into this mess; yet now, looking back, he wondered if he'd ever had a choice. Once he'd laid eyes on her, there was something inside him that *knew*, because once he'd laid eyes on her, life had become bearable again.

"Ask it," he almost growled, when her silence had become more than he could stand.

Feeling slightly sick, she let her hand drift to her stomach. She didn't want to know, but she had to. Maureen's type of illness couldn't have lasted this long.

"Ask it!" he provoked.

"All right," she whispered. "When? When did she die?"

"Almost two years ago." He had to look away from the stricken expression that crossed her face. "You don't understand. The insurance ran dry, and I've been stuck paying her medical bills. I sold the house and practically everything in it, but there was still a hefty balance left to pay. I even took another job as a security guard to move things along faster. It's been my preoccupation day and night."

"Did you think me so mercenary that I'd only want to be with you if you were solvent?" she demanded incredulously. "Did you think it mattered to me?"

"It mattered to me!"

"Congratulations," she muttered. "I hope you and your stubborn pride are very happy together!"

She couldn't believe she said that, or that they were doing this to each other. Enough! She needed to get out of there. Pivoting on her heels, she headed for the stairs.

"Wait!"

Kendall hesitated at the bottom step, then turned around. She didn't even bother to lie to herself about why. She was putty in his hands; couldn't he see that? His talk of pride was Greek to her. She'd used whatever pride she'd had on that one gesture of leaving Houston.

Braden took a step toward her. "It wasn't just pride that kept me away," he began, his voice raw. "It was guilt. Kendall...it got to the point I almost *wanted* her to die. What kind of man did that make me?" His chest rose and fell. "And so, afterward, I became obsessed with her bills. Call it penance, I don't know. I just had to do it."

"But what you experienced was normal, Braden. Anyone who'd been through that kind of ordeal would have felt the same way. You're only human." She took a tentative step closer. "The important thing is that you were there with her when she needed you."

"I think she despised me in the end."

"I doubt that. She was ill and probably feeling a little cheated and scared. Maybe you just represented a reminder of what wasn't to be."

Braden closed his eyes against a searing pain of longing. When he reopened them, he stared at her with an expression that made her breath lock in her throat.

"You're intent on finding some redeeming quality in me, aren't you?" he said harshly.

"I don't happen to believe it's a difficult task."

"Henry didn't want me to come. He thought... maybe there'd be someone else. Is there?"

She shook her head, her eyes brimming with dreams. "I guess I could never quite get you out of my system."

"Stop trying."

In two long strides he covered the distance between them and swept her up into his arms. In the next heartbeat he crushed his mouth down onto hers.

"Baby..." Braden's whispers of adoration were interspersed with near-frantic kisses trailing across her cheek, to her ear, down the silken length of her neck. His touch wasn't quite gentle: it was restless, as if he had to touch her everywhere immediately, molding her to his aching body.

"Touching you makes me crazy," he said huskily.

"And me," she whispered, wanting his mouth on hers again, and pulling his head back to her face. "Kiss me. I'm so hungry for you."

His body shook at her breathless confession. This time he took her mouth more carefully, but with the same intense need. Their shuddering breaths mingled, their tongues parried and tempted as Braden slid his hands down to her buttocks and perfected their closeness.

Kendall felt her insides melt away as she whimpered against him. Tremors of excitement ignited deep within her and spread like fire throughout her body. Nothing she'd ever experienced had felt quite like this. He made a mockery of every man she'd ever known.

"Braden," she moaned, burying her face in his shoulder as he moved against her again.

"I know...I know..." There was a brief, tense silence as he fought to win back control. "I have to stop touching you, or I'm going to take you right on this carpet."

"Ask me to stand right now, and I'll sink straight to my knees," she countered with a shaky laugh. She felt his smile as he brushed his lips against her warm brow.

"Your effect on me is just as lethal," he murmured.

But his attempt to lighten things between them was short-lived when he looked into her eyes a moment later. He couldn't restrain himself from touching her, tasting her, and once he started toying with the delicate folds of her ear, his body began to throb again.

"It's no good," he said thickly. "I want you too much."

"I want you, too."

"We should talk, though."

"Sure...me first." She drew his mouth down to her parted lips, caressing him and luring him into the sweet cavern of her mouth. Then she melted for him.

It was more than he could take, more than any man should be asked to resist. Passion flowed between them escalating into a steamy heat. He knew already that they weren't going to make it upstairs, but he'd make it good for her. If not the first time...

"Braden...I hear bells."

Bells were good. Sweet, like her. But he wanted the ultimate for her—rocket explosions.

"Braden?"

Damned if he wasn't beginning to hear them, too. He raised his head and frowned. Then the frown turned into a wry grin. "The phone."

"The what?"

Her eyes were glassy, dazed. He chuckled softly and kissed the tip of her small, straight nose. "It's the *telephone*."

"Ah."

She wobbled a little when he set her back onto her feet. Letting her slide down against his hard body was unfair torture. She shot him a look that promised retaliation, then concentrated on trying to remember where the phone was.

"Hello," she murmured into the kitchen extension, silently hoping it wasn't her partner, Frank. He never had gotten around to finishing that awful joke he'd started during lunch. It would be just like him to... "Hello?"

She frowned and looked up to see Braden watching her. A silent message passed between them, and a faint chill ran down her spine. She listened a moment longer, then slowly hung up.

"Well?"

"There was no one there."

"Does that happen often?"

She knew what he meant: did she receive many crank calls? But just about any call in their vicinity would be considered a toll call, so pranksters were few and far between.

"No," she replied. She didn't like the white line that was forming around his compressed lips or the coldness returning to his eyes. "It could have been a wrong number. Lots of people hang up when they get a wrong number, never saying a word."

"Is that what happened? Did the person on the other end hang up?"

"Well, no. But—"

"Kendall—"

"It couldn't have been *him*!" she insisted. "It's too soon. You've barely gotten here yourself. I can't believe his sources could outdo yours."

"I'd like nothing better than to agree with you, but it's a luxury we can't afford." He rubbed the back of his neck and blew out a gust of breath in frustration. "Beautiful," he growled. "I should just unlock the doors and lay out a welcome mat for all the good I'm doing."

"What are you talking about?"

"I'm poison to you! I always have been."

"That's not true!"

"Oh, yeah? There's a nut out there who wants to kill us because I was forced to shoot his brother," Braden snapped, pointing outside. "How's that for starters? And here I am, supposedly to warn you and help stop him, and all I can think of is making love to you." He swore softly, thrusting one hand on his hip, and the other through his hair. "Henry was right. Where you're concerned, my objectivity takes a flying leap."

Kendall couldn't keep from smiling. "Did he say that?"

"Hell, no. He wasn't as polite."

Edging closer, Kendall laid a soothing hand on his chest, but Braden grabbed hold of her wrist. Still, he couldn't quite bring himself to push her away. "I've already proved that my resistance to you is virtually nonexistent, so help me out, okay? If that phone hadn't rung, I'd be so wrapped around you by now that Lockwood could come through the front door with a tank, and I wouldn't give a damn." He took a ragged breath as he watched her moist lips part. "Kendall, as sure as I believe in heaven, I know there's got to be a time for us, but it can't be now. Not until this thing with Lockwood is settled . . . and not until you've had a chance to think about things and know for sure that I'm what you want."

"How could you believe otherwise?"

He gave her a brief, thoroughly masculine smile. "I mean besides sex. I know I can make you want me physically. I think, subconsciously, I've been working on that from the moment I set eyes on you. I'm no saint.

"I'm talking about the rest of it, Kendall. The—"

Kendall placed her fingertips against his lips to silence him. "There'll be no more talk about the past if it includes the word *guilt*, do you hear me?"

He trapped her fingers within his and brushed his lips against the back of her hand. "There's something else I'd like you to know. I've been faithful to you since the day I kissed you."

Kendall stared at him, stunned.

"Didn't you think I had it in me?" he mocked gently.

"Yes...no...I—I'm not sure," she stammered. It was the one thing she'd never let herself dwell on, knowing it would have been the surest route to insanity. He was a virile man. There were a lot of women— several she remembered from their old precinct— who'd have been more than content to settle for a one-night stand and not give a second thought to whether he'd been married or not.

"I didn't want a body; I wanted you," he said, as if reading her mind. Gently he brushed her hair away from her cheek. "Only you."

Kendall's eyes drifted closed. "Make love to me," she begged softly.

When had he ever heard anything half so beautiful? Braden took in every inch of her face with hungry eyes, knowing he'd want to remember this moment for the rest of his life, then forced himself to move away from her.

"Say that to me again when this is over, and I promise you won't get out of bed for a week."

In mutinous silence she watched as he went to turn off the kitchen light and retrieve his things. "You're a hard man, Braden Manning," she pronounced at last, unaware of how accurate she really was.

Braden cleared his throat and maneuvered his jacket to where it would do the most good. "Come on, *partner*," he coaxed. "Get these lights off, and let's turn in. If that was Lockwood on the phone, he's been moving damned fast and is probably too beat to try anything tonight. That should allow us to get at least one good night of sleep."

He must be joking, Kendall thought, grabbing her purse from the kitchen table. Sleep? Who could possibly sleep after all this? She turned on the stairway lights and then went back to help him get the table lamps. As she started back upstairs, Braden laid a restraining hand on her arm.

"If I promise you can exact revenge at a later date, can I have a smile?" he asked, his look warm.

Unable to resist him, her lips curved sweetly. "I *am* glad you're here." She sighed. "Frustrated, but glad."

"Likewise, green eyes. Do you still carry a thirty-eight?"

In response she opened her purse and pulled out the revolver she was required to carry at all times.

"Good. From here on out, keep it close."

"Yes. I know."

A few minutes later her fingers touched the cool metal tucked beneath the pillow beside her. With a sigh she settled more comfortably in her bed and stared up into the darkness. Inevitably she turned her head toward the wall that separated her from Braden.

The day had evolved beyond anything she could possibly have imagined: not all of it good, by any means. Royce...Maureen...It all made her head spin. But she felt a giddiness, too, something that she would have normally associated with adolescent romance. There were a thousand and one things she wanted to ask Braden, talk to him about. She wanted to touch him and love him and just plain look at him.

He was back in her life...and free. The future suddenly bubbled with excitement and possibilities.

And to think that one disturbed man played the pivotal role in bringing it all about. The same man was all that stood between Kendall and Braden and their happiness, and he wanted to deprive them of it.

"Please," she whispered into the darkness. "Give it up, Royce. Just give it up."

Four

Was it the scream that awoke her or the resounding crash? Kendall sat up in bed and quickly decided that either way she'd better investigate.

Without a thought to her attire, she scrambled out of bed, snatching up her revolver as she went. The sound of angry voices came from downstairs. She raced past Braden's room and the bathroom glancing quickly inside. Both were empty. She took the stairs with lithe but precarious speed.

Her heart was pounding, and adrenaline was flowing when she whipped around the corner of the kitchen, her revolver raised and ready. Braden and Bruno stopped arguing immediately.

"Kendall—you too mit de guns!" Bruno cried, his round face flushed. "Vat goes on here?"

He stood pressed up against the back door, with Braden standing before him. On the floor between them lay a broken platter, and from beneath it oozed what Kendall could only guess had been a cake. Despite the fact that Braden's gun was now lowered to his side, Bruno's hands remained high in surrender.

"Oh, no," Kendall moaned. She lowered her gun, set it on the table and scurried barefoot across the linoleum floor to join them. "Bruno, are you okay? You can put your hands down. Come in and sit down." She patted his arm gently. "What's that? Chocolate torte?"

"Not anymore," the portly chef replied, dolefully eyeing his culinary creation.

Kendall bit her lip to repress a smile. They stepped over the mess, and she got Bruno settled in a chair. "All right," she said, turning back to Braden and planting her hand on her hips. "What happened?"

His left brow arched at her tone of voice. "What do you think happened? I thought he was breaking in."

"Breaking in—Braden, this is my *neighbor*." She went through quick introductions, but it was easy to see that the two men weren't exactly ready to become friends.

"Kendall, you are having some trouble?" Bruno asked, concern mirrored in his gentle brown eyes.

"A little, but it's nothing for you to be concerned about."

"I can help, *ja*?"

"He can help, *no*!" muttered Braden.

"Bruno, everything's under control, really," Kendall interjected quickly. "We're only watching for a man who may come around here to cause a little trouble. The best help you could provide would be to keep your doors locked, and if you should happen to see anything peculiar, call me, or the police, right away."

"But of course. Er—does this mean then that you cannot take my boy, Fritz? Remember? The seminar in Dallas?"

"Oh, that's right. I'd forgotten. You leave in the morning, don't you? I'll be happy to have him stay here," she said, ignoring Braden's urgent signals to her to say no. "And don't worry: I'll take good care of him."

Bruno politely declined the invitation to stay for coffee, fussed with her over who should clean up the mess, and after she apologized again for the plate, said a stiff goodbye to Braden and left. Kendall waved until he was back in his car, then closed the screen door.

She and Braden exchanged glares. "How could you?" she demanded. "That sweet little man wouldn't hurt a fly. You could've given him a heart attack!"

"What about *me*? I heard a car, footsteps, and someone at the door. How was I to know you get international cuisine delivered at the crack of dawn?" Scowling, he leaned back against the counter and folded his arms across his chest. "And by the way, Kendall, let's get something straight right away. We are not baby-sitting any children. It's too much of a risk."

Kendall paused from trying to scoop up most of the cake between the two platter halves. "What children?"

"Bruno's son, Fritz!"

Her eyes rolled heavenward. "Fritz is Bruno's Airedale terrier." She carried the remnants of the cake to the garbage and then went to the sink to wash her hands. A second later she felt Braden's arms slide around her, and she was pulled back against his body.

"I guess this is where I apologize," he said sighing.

A smile tugged at her lips. "You did overreact."

"Guilty." He buried his face in her sleep-mussed hair. "But you're partly to blame, you know."

"Oh-ho! This should be interesting. How do you figure that?"

"If you hadn't come downstairs looking like the sexiest avenging angel I'd ever seen, I would have kept my head...maybe even invited old Bruno for coffee myself, once I figured out who he was. But a man's blood pressure can only take so much."

"Some backup I'd be if I stopped to change," she mused. "Besides, this football jersey is perfectly respectable. What's wrong with it?"

"Nothing that a quick leap into the Arctic Ocean wouldn't cure," he said, biting at her neck softly.

Kendall's eyes drifted closed in pleasure as his stroking fingers inched up along her ribs and began seeking the gentle swell of her breasts. She hadn't been able to avoid missing what he looked like, either. Wearing jeans and nothing else, he looked wonderful. He'd lost none of the muscle tone he'd perfected in college. His arms, shoulders and chest were magnificent, and the dark forest of hair tapering from his chest down to, and beyond, the snap of his jeans made her fingertips itch to follow. She wriggled in his arms, trying to turn to face him, but he wouldn't let her.

"Are you going to tell me?"

"Give me a hint of what we're talking about first."

"Who do you know at Notre Dame?"

"Ah, we're back to the jersey again." She sighed, loving the feel of his mouth on her skin.

"Correction, we're *still* on the damned jersey."

"My, we are cranky in the morning, aren't we?" She yelped as his touch became ticklish. "Okay, okay! I don't know anyone there. I just bought it on sale last year. It's comfortable to sleep in…and it reminds me of you."

"I should have known," he groaned, hugging her closer. "Forgive me?"

"For what?"

He chuckled softly. "Lady, I'm going to like arguing with you."

"We didn't argue. We never argue."

"You used to say the same thing when we were partners. But I'll tell you what. If we can make up like this from now on, I'll call it whatever you want."

Kendall was no longer listening. She covered his hands with her own and urged them closer to where she ached the most. "Braden," she whispered. "Touch me."

He hadn't meant to start this, but now that he had, he wasn't ready to let her go. His big callused hands slid over her breasts. A shudder swept through him as he felt her grow warm and firm beneath his fingers. He stroked her lazily with his thumbs. "I want to put my mouth there."

"I'd let you." She lifted her arms behind her to encircle his neck. "And then I'd do it to you."

Behind his closed lids Braden could picture it—and more—and a sweet pain twisted inside him. How he needed her, wanted her. It had been too long since he'd been with a woman, and she was too potent an aphrodisiac.

With something close to a growl, he kissed her fiercely and then pushed her to arm's length.

"What—" Kendall turned, bewildered.

"I'll start the coffee and finish cleaning the floor. Go on upstairs and put some decent clothes on."

She blinked owlishly.

"Out, woman."

He wasn't...he couldn't be doing this to her again. She couldn't believe it. "Braden, I'll get you for this!"

He grabbed the coffeepot, not at all surprised to see it shake in his hand. "I'll look forward to it," he replied gruffly. "Now get, while I can still remember why I'm doing this."

Twenty minutes later, fresh from a shower and with her hair almost blow-dried, Kendall's frustration had abated enough to allow her to put things into a clearer perspective. It wouldn't be fair of her to be annoyed with him: after all, this couldn't be easy on him, either. It wasn't his fault they set grass fires whenever they were within ten feet of each other. The memory of how he'd felt pressed against her back sent a warm flame licking along her inner thighs.

Determinedly she shook her head. She had to get a hold of herself, or she wasn't going to be any help to him at all. He was right: Royce was the one they needed to be concentrating on. The price they could pay for not keeping that in mind was one she couldn't bear to think about. If that was why Braden was putting his own needs and desires aside, the least she could do was not make things more difficult than they already were.

As she studied her reflection in the bathroom mirror, she thought of the other reason for his self-imposed celibacy and his decision not to break it. What a contradiction he was. He was so sure of his own feelings, but not of hers. It was understandable, she supposed, considering the fact that the subject hadn't come up for discussion—not back then, or now. Once they'd realized what was happening between them they'd worked hard to avoid it. And last night there had been more than enough to take in. Kendall smiled ruefully. No one could accuse Father Time of giving them preferential treatment.

She switched off her hair dryer and unplugged it. There was no question but that the past had made Braden cautious. His unhappy marriage, and his guilt in the end, all worked together to do a hatchet job on his self-esteem. She didn't think it was fair. As much as she sympathized with Maureen for her untimely death, she was disappointed in her, as well. Kendall passionately believed that a life spent in anger was a wasted life, and she was afraid that Maureen's last years were spent just that way.

Standing back from the mirror, Kendall took a last look at her appearance. Her gaze drifted over her white scoop-neck T-shirt and powder-blue jeans. Thoughtfully her fingers brushed over her flat stomach. Braden had once mentioned his desire for children and his frustration with Maureen for putting them off. She would give him a child gladly. She turned sideways and tried unsuccessfully to stick out her stomach. A soft laugh bubbled up from her throat. A baby...Braden's baby...the thought made her tingle all over. She'd never allowed herself to dream of it; yet more than anything, she wanted a family of her own to cherish, where no member would ever doubt that they were wanted and loved.

"Hey, up there! If I go through the trouble of cooking breakfast, the least you can do is come down and eat it."

Laughing, Kendall stepped out of the bathroom and peered over the railing. Braden grinned up at her. It took years off his face, and with the blue plaid shirt he'd put on, she thought he was gorgeous. Oh, yes, she told herself, everything was going to be fine.

She ran lightly down the stairs. "If I smelled bacon or sausage frying, I'd have been down..." She stopped before the kitchen table and stared down at the platter of peanut butter and jelly sandwiches. "What's this?" she asked incredulously.

"Breakfast."

"Uh-huh." She gave him a dry look over her shoulder. "I distinctly heard the word cooking. 'Cooking breakfast,' you said."

"Yeah? Must be bad acoustics or something." His grin had a boyish appeal to it. "Actually, I can't cook," he confessed. "And you didn't have any TV dinners in the freezer, so..."

"I get the picture."

"What's the matter? Did you want them on crackers instead?"

"Ah, nope. White bread is just dandy with me." How could she complain when he was so obviously eager to please her? "But aren't there an awful lot of sandwiches here?"

He gallantly helped her into her chair. "I'm hungry. This body takes a lot of fuel to keep it going."

Of course. There was no forgetting the enormous lunches he used to order, and how, after he was finished with his, he'd always have room to polish off what was left of hers. "You should have let me make you breakfast," she said, feeling guilty.

"Well, I knew we'd have to go into town to talk to your people," he hedged.

"Sure. But not at this hour. When was your last cooked meal?"

"Don't ask." He took his own seat and grabbed a sandwich. "Listen, I'll be more than happy to let you cook to your heart's content after this, but I just wanted to do something.... Well, damn, like you said, this hasn't been easy for you."

Was it possible, wondered Kendall, to love somebody more with every passing minute? "That's sweet,
but as you pointed out, this situation isn't your fault."

"I was referring mainly to the way I reacted with
your friend, Bruno, and that guy last night."

"Adam."

"Adam," he repeated eyeing his sandwich menac-
ingly.

"Adam Rhodes. He's the D.A. here in town."

Braden's teeth sank into the white bread as though
he were about to chomp a brick in half. "Right. Well,
maybe I acted a bit Neanderthal."

"You're jealous."

"Yeah." He sighed. "Always have been of you.
You don't know what it was like to watch people hov-
ering around you like hummingbirds to one special
flower. I was proud, but I was also jealous, because I
always expected one of them to take away what little
of you I had."

He didn't notice that a bit of jelly remained at the
corner of his mouth, but Kendall did. She leaned over
to dab it away with the tip of her finger, then licked it
clean. Watching her pink tongue disappear, Braden's
mouth went dry.

"Thank you for telling me that," she said quietly.
"But weren't you listening last night when I told you
that there wasn't anyone else in my life?"

Oh, he'd heard, all right. He'd replayed that moment over and over again in his mind, savoring it each
time.

"I thought that was why you confessed later about not having been with anyone either since—" She broke off, a little embarrassed.

Either. His eyes widened. *"Either?"*

Kendall shook her head slowly. "You still don't understand, do you?"

Their gazes held. The sandwich fell from Braden's hands. Slowly he rose from his chair, dropped to his knees beside her and drew her around to face him. His hand lifted tentatively to her hair, then fell away.

"I gave up dreaming a long time ago," he began, his voice marked with suppressed emotion. "The cost just got too high. I have to tell you that if this thing with Lockwood hadn't come up, I might never have come after you. I couldn't believe that someone hadn't already swept you away, and there was a part of me that sincerely wanted you to have that chance if it was what you wanted."

"Braden," she whispered achingly.

"I'm still not convinced that I'm what you need. God knows, you deserve better."

"Don't start that again; it just isn't true."

His hands gripped her small waist. "Hush. Let me get it all out, once and for all.

"That was the noble part of me, but I'm a pretty selfish bastard, as well. The other guys have had their chance, and I'm not fool enough to give them another. I've got six more months of abject poverty to ride out, but if what I see in those big, beautiful eyes isn't wishful thinking on my part, I'll spend the rest of my life trying to make you not regret waiting for me."

Tears spilled from Kendall's eyes. "I love you so much."

Braden didn't need to hear any more. He slid his hands into her hair and claimed her mouth in a kiss that was both ravishing and sweet. It tasted of peanut butter, tears and jelly. They couldn't help but laugh.

"We may be on to something here," he teased. Gently, with feathery kisses, he caught up her tears. "Ah, love, don't cry."

"I can't help it," she sniffed. "What you said was so beautiful."

His silvery eyes gleamed possessively. "I love you. I guess that can change even a lost cause like me."

He brushed his lips across hers, then took full possession. Blood surged wildly through his head and body. She was a drug, and he was addicted, and he knew he'd spend the rest of his life trying to get enough of her. Her name was an aching whisper on his lips as their kiss went from worshiping to passionate.

They both jumped when the front doorbell rang. Then their eyes met, and they burst into laughter again, feeling like two teenagers caught necking.

Braden's laughter ended on a groan. He sat back on his heels, raking his hands through his hair. "Somebody has lousy timing," he muttered, checking his watch. "Isn't it still a bit early for company?"

"You mean even for me?" She smiled. "I wasn't expecting anyone." But the next series of rings ended on an impatient knocking and had them both rising.

"Wait a second." Braden grabbed his gun from the holster he'd brought down when he went for his shirt.

"I'm coming with you." They moved quietly to the front door, and as Braden positioned himself behind it, Kendall peered through the small security hole.

"Frank—" she murmured in surprise. She barely released the dead bolt and turned the doorknob when a raven-haired man burst in. "Frank!"

He hugged her fiercely. "Five seconds more, and I was going to kick the door in. I don't know whether to spank you or kiss you."

"My suggestion is neither," Braden replied tersely from behind him.

Frank went very still. Slowly he released Kendall, careful to keep his hands visible. "I sure hope you're Manning," he drawled. His dark eyes, however, were sharp and questioning as they drilled into Kendall.

"It's all right," she assured him. "Braden, this is my partner, Frank Ortega. Frank, Braden Manning, which somehow you've already surmised."

Frank turned, his black slashing brows lifting subtly as he noticed the nine millimeter being expertly tucked away. Several inches shorter and as many years younger, he had neither Braden's massive shoulder span, nor his muscular build, but there was a fluid, relaxed quality about him that suggested a different type of strength: skills that could make him as dangerous as Braden. Dressed in jeans, a white shirt and a navy windbreaker—which undoubtedly covered his own gun—he gave an immediate impression of confidence and caution.

He appeared to approve of what he saw in Braden. Grinning, his white teeth a bright flash of white against his olive skin, he said, "You have a talent for letting a man know he's got a gun in his back."

"That's because my boss gets upset when I waste bullets."

Frank laughed and nodded. "You're Manning, all right. They warned me that your sense of humor was double-edged." He winked at Kendall. "And that your loyalty to friends was unwavering. So is mine." He extended his hand. "Pleased to meet you."

Only after Braden accepted it did Kendall release her long-held breath. "Well, now that a second Alamo has been averted, would you mind telling me what you're doing here, Frank? And who told you about Braden?"

"Does the name Fielder mean anything to you? He phoned headquarters awhile ago and asked for whoever was in charge. When he learned it was Simpson—whom, it turned out, he knew, or something—he phoned him at home." He turned back to Braden. "Your Captain Fielder says he's going to be away for a while—another crisis or something—and he'll contact you later. Anyway, when Simpson heard what was going on, he phoned me right away. Since I only live a few miles up the road, I told him I'd check things out."

"Doesn't anybody believe in using the phone anymore?" Kendall complained.

"About as much as you do," countered Frank. He took her by the shoulders. "Kendall, you should have called me right away."

"No lectures, please. I only learned about Royce myself late last night, and Braden was here. If I had to put up any more cops for the night, I might as well have gone down to the station to sleep."

"Okay," Frank relented. "But Simpson said you were to get your cute tush downtown by eleven sharp for a complete review of the situation, and I'm coming along."

"Uh-uh."

"I'm in on this, North."

Kendall's veto was vehement. "No way, my friend. You've got a pregnant wife at home who doesn't need you pulling special duty on top of everything else."

"Ginger is one hundred percent behind me on this."

"Oh, really? Well, tell Ginger she doesn't get a vote!"

Braden came up behind her and gently grasped her shoulders. "It might not be a bad idea. It's wishful thinking to expect that they'll let us handle this completely on our own. If we have to have backup, I'd prefer to have someone around that you trust."

"Now wait a minute," Kendall protested. "You have to understand—"

"I knew there was something about him I liked," Frank said with a chuckle. He tucked his hands into the back pockets of his jeans and rocked back on the heels of his boots.

"Don't get a swollen head, Ortega. I think what he likes about you is finding out about that pregnant wife," Kendall drawled, shooting Braden a dry look. His answering smile was predatory.

Frank intercepted the exchange, and his eyes narrowed with interest. "What's this? Well, I'll be...Angel face, have you been two-timing me?"

"Ortega, don't do me any favors, okay? And if you get a black eye, I'm giving you fair warning that I am not going to help you explain it to Ginger."

Frank mimicked a painful wince, then, abruptly, he pulled her into his arms for a bear hug. Over her shoulder he grinned at Braden. "You going to make an honest woman of her?"

"Frank!"

"We were discussing it when we were interrupted by your untimely visit," Braden said. When Kendall looked back at him, for a moment it was as if there were just the two of them in the room. "Why don't we go into the kitchen and talk over coffee," he said thickly. "Breakfast is getting cold. What do you think about peanut butter and jelly, Frank?"

Several hours later it was a subdued Braden and Kendall who drove back to the house.

"You still don't like it, do you?"

Kendall opened her eyes. His voice broke through her thoughts, perfectly capsulizing them.

She blinked at the sun glaring through the windshield of his Mustang. They were almost back to her house. Fewer and fewer stores and houses dotted the sandy, uneven terrain. The hot July wind felt good against her skin as it blew in the open windows.

No, she didn't like it, and that was ironic, since it was her idea that they settled on in the end. She'd sat there in Simpson's office, listening to them all arguing, tossing around one idea after another. Finally, she'd deduced that the simplest, safest way for Frank to be their backup was to put him in the Cheeseys' house. She had their keys during their absence, and she was in and out of there all the time tending plants or dropping off their mail. Its location was ideal, and the timers which were placed on the lights already suggested that someone was home. She wasn't surprised at all when everyone agreed. So why did it still bother her?

"Kendall?"

"Hmm? Oh . . . sorry. What did you say?"

"Your neighbors . . . you're not worried that they'll be upset or disapprove, are you?"

"No. If I thought that, I wouldn't have made the suggestion in the first place. No, they're great people. In fact they'll probably decide they missed all the excitement and wish they'd stayed home."

Braden smiled crookedly. "Helluva name, Cheesey."

"Yeah."

He glanced at her profile. "It's Frank, isn't it?"

Give the man a cigar. She sighed inwardly. "He and Ginger are my friends," she began. "When I first arrived here and he and I became partners, they weren't married yet, but anyone could see that they were wildly in love. She was all he ever talked about. Frank had had a pretty rough life. He's literally dragged himself up from squalor, and between his sensitivity over that and his Latin temperament, he built a reputation for not being the easiest person on the force to work with. Ginger has really mellowed him, and when he starts talking about the baby..." She dropped her head back against the seat and closed her eyes. "I only hope that nothing goes wrong, because I couldn't handle it if he got hurt because of me."

"He'll be fine. He can take care of himself."

"He's a good cop," she agreed. "I'd trust him with my life."

"You do every day you're riding together."

"Yes, but—" She bit her lip, struggling for the right words. "This is different. It feels... personal; therefore, I feel it's wrong for him to take any risks on my behalf. His responsibility is to Ginger and their baby."

"That's not how it works, and you know it. We don't have any neat lines separating our professional and private lives. That's why we keep divorce lawyers so busy. All the lines cross. It's an occupational hazard. Today you need help; tomorrow he might. If it happened that he was in trouble, even if it was something out of his past, wouldn't you go to him?"

"I guess."

"So?"

"So I don't have a wife who's seven-and-a-half months pregnant," she muttered, her logic having gone full circle. "So sue me for feeling guilty."

Braden reached across the seat, took her hand and brought it to his lips. "I'd rather love you," he murmured, kissing her again. He meant it to be a fleeting kiss, but the softness of her skin and the light fragrance it carried lured him into a prolonged caress.

Kendall's pulse began to throb, and she knew he could feel it. "You do know how to change the subject, don't you?" she said quietly, peering from beneath her long, velvety lashes.

He only smiled. As they approached her driveway, he asked her if she wanted him to check for mail.

"Yes, please . . . and the Cheeseys', too."

He handed her the mail from her box, and while he checked next door, she leafed through the small stack. She paused when she came to a rather dirty folded sheet of paper.

"Looks like those generators of junk mail have achieved a new low," she mused, unfolding the sheet out of sheer curiosity. The sardonic grin on her face faltered a moment later.

"What did you get, a ten-percent-off coupon for the local massage parlor?"

"I wish it was."

"Say that again," he said with a laugh, turning to hand her the Cheeseys' mail. Her face was paste white, and held the strangest look. Abruptly he dropped the mail he was holding and grabbed the sheet from out of her hand. There were only two words, and they were hastily scrawled, but two words were enough.

It's time.

Braden swore bitterly.

Five

Well, there goes the neighborhood," Kendall said, opting for humor, weak as it was.

"There goes your speculation on whether he'd show up or not," countered Braden grimly.

She scanned the area, as he did, looking for a sign, movement, anything. The potted flowers on her front porch danced merrily in the light breeze. Behind the house the waves rolled in, one after the other, with calm indifference. Everywhere they looked, they received the same anticlimactic picture—serenity and welcome.

"Do you think he's still around?" she asked.

"I don't know, but I do know being like this makes me feel like a sitting duck. Keep your eyes open—I'm taking us in."

Kendall pulled out her revolver from her purse and released her seat belt; however, they made it in without incident. "You want to check around the house before we go in?" she suggested as he shut off the engine.

"Yeah. You go around the back, and I'll go around the front."

A moment or two later they were back at his car. "There aren't any signs of attempted forced entry," she said, shading her eyes to study Bruno's house and then the dunes again. "Maybe the note was it."

"Maybe. Let's get these groceries inside before they melt."

They'd stopped to restock Kendall's refrigerator on the way home. It had been agreed upon that they'd keep a low profile for the next few days and stay inside as much as possible. The brief excursion to the grocery store had been fun as they compared likes and dislikes, but now their mood was somber as they collected the sacks and hurried inside.

"What in the world...?" Kendall stepped into her kitchen, and a stifling heat engulfed her. "My air conditioner... *oh, not now!*" She quickly set her bag on the counter and ran to check the register in the living room. When she returned, her expression mirrored her confusion. "I don't get it. I can hear the motor running, but it's got to be over ninety in here."

"Shut it off," Braden directed. "I'll take a look outside." He didn't like the vibes he was getting. If Lockwood had been to the mailbox, there was no telling what else he'd been up to.

Kendall was waiting for him at the door when he returned. "That bad, huh?" she murmured, observing his grim expression.

"He ruptured the copper tubing carrying the Freon. You'll have to have a repairman come out; and seeing that it's the weekend and their busiest season, guess how easy that's going to be?"

"He's certainly giving this some thought."

"He's playing games." Braden went to the living room to turn on the ceiling fan and began opening the windows. "He wanted a window of vulnerability, and now he's got one," he muttered in disgust. "In fact, the way it looks, he'll have his choice." He swore again softly and headed for the stairs.

Kendall grabbed his arm. "He's getting to you," she warned.

Braden took a calming breath. "This isn't what I expected," he admitted. "I expected him to be immediately confrontational."

"I know. But obviously he has other plans." She took his hand and led him back down the stairs. "Darling, don't you see what he's trying to do? Obviously he knows you're here, and it's a little more than he counted on. So now he has to separate us. If he can't do it physically, he'll try psychologically... heat, tempers, paranoia. Getting you angry is a start; next he'll have us going at each other. It's exactly what he wants. Please, let's not give him the satisfaction." She moved closer, slipping her arms around his waist. Going on tiptoe, she kissed his chin, then his lips, smiling as she felt the tension flow from him.

"You're right," he sighed. "You're right." He folded her closer and kissed her brow. "It's the thought of something happening to you, when I've only just found you again. I can't afford to let this dream we've begun to weave together turn to ashes like the rest. Do you understand? I can't."

"It won't happen," she assured him, her eyes adoring.

He lowered his head, needing the taste of her refreshed on his lips. When he raised it a moment later, he hurt all over, and there were tears in her eyes. He bent to kiss her lids closed when the phone rang.

"Go away," Kendall grumbled.

Braden smiled. "Let me get it. It might be Fielder."

Kendall followed him into the kitchen, intent on putting the rest of the groceries away, but it soon became obvious that it wasn't Captain Fielder on the phone. Braden curtly asked the party to hold and handed her the receiver.

"It's your friend the D.A.," he muttered. "Would you mind assuring him that I'm not an ax-murderer and that you're all right."

"Adam?" she began hesitantly. "Hi, what's up?"

"What's up?" he fumed. "North, do you realize that I've been trying to reach you all morning? The things that have been going through my mind..."

"It's the company you keep," she sympathized. "Your psyche is programmed to look for guilt. I told you I'd be fine."

"Never mind my psyche, and never mind what you said; do you know I was about to call Simpson?"

"Well, you should have," she replied cheerfully. "We could have talked, then, since I was in his office all morning." He muttered something indecipherable. "I'm sorry, Adam, really I am. What's the matter?" she asked mischievously. "Did worrying about me mess up your concentration on the golf course today?"

"You know it did. I had to pick up Judge Perry's lunch *and* his martini bill."

Kendall clucked sympathetically. "But I'm sure you'll recover that one way or another," she added.

"Brat," he grumbled good-naturedly. Then he did that head-spinning switch on her that was so effective in the courtroom. "What were you doing in Simpson's office...on a Saturday...during your vacation?"

"Whoa," she protested. "How did I suddenly land up on the witness stand?"

"If I think someone's being fast on their feet, I have to be faster. Now what's going on, Kendall? Out with it."

She filled him in, albeit reluctantly. She knew him well enough to know that if she didn't he'd have no compunctions about calling Simpson for the information, and she went through enough kidding about the variety and devotion of her friends without *that*.

He whistled softly at the end of her story. "No wonder what's-his-name was ready to pounce on me last night. Maybe I owe him an apology."

"Shall I put him on the phone?" she asked sweetly.

"Another time, perhaps. More importantly, tell me what I can do to help."

"Nothing."

He made a sound of frustration. "Has he called, made any threats? What about a wiretap or trace?"

"We did receive one call last night," she admitted. "But there was no way to be sure if it was him, so we're holding off on both until we can make a positive ID. You know what a hassle it is to get the paperwork done on those things, and then to get them signed by a judge and the phone company... and on a weekend, no less."

"I can save you time there. If you decide to go that route, call me—day or night—understand?" He briefly ran through his schedule with her and hung up promising to check in with his service for phone messages on the hour.

Kendall replaced the receiver and went into Braden's extended arms. She told him about Adam's offer.

"He was really worried, wasn't he?" When she nodded, he hugged her closer. "I'm glad that you've had such good friends to be here for you when I couldn't." There was a long trembling silence between them, and then he said thickly, "You know what would be a good idea? Why don't you go on upstairs, get the windows and change into something lighter. It's going to stay pretty hot in here, and I don't want your temper doing what mine almost did."

"I suppose. What about you?"

"I'll ditch my shirt . . . that is, if you can handle the temptation?"

She laughed softly. "Probably not, but I doubt you'll let me do anything about it, will you?"

To her surprise he neither smiled nor tossed back a glib reply. Instead he frowned. "Kendall—you do understand why it's important for us to have this time and space, don't you?"

"Yes. I don't necessarily like it, or agree—except for the part about concentrating on Royce—but I understand. And if it'll make you feel any better, I respect you for it. You make me feel . . . special."

"You are." Out of the corner of his eye he saw the now familiar blue pickup truck drive by, and reluctantly he released her. "There goes Frank. When he gets settled next door, I'll raise him on the radio and fill him in on the latest."

For the next hour or so they stayed busy. After Kendall changed into loose shorts and a white eyelet camisole top, she brushed her hair into a ponytail to keep the back of her neck cooler. When she came back downstairs, she tackled the rest of the groceries, and then looked up an air-conditioner repairman in the yellow pages. Just as Braden warned, the recorded message said they were booked up with service calls, but that if she'd leave her name and number someone would get back to her as soon as possible. She did and went on to start dinner. After Braden spoke to Frank, he went outside and redirected the floodlights into a position that would allow optimum use.

They decided to eat dinner on the living room floor while watching the evening news. The intimate arrangement was marred only by the fact that each of them had their guns within reaching distance. Every few minutes their eyes would be drawn to each other's, and they'd exchange smiles.

Someday all our moments will be like this, Kendall thought contentedly. She enjoyed the idea of planning meals and shopping for two. Her gaze focused on the steak she was shoving around on her plate, and with a wry smile put down her fork. Now if only she could develop an appetite.

"I see your eating habits haven't changed."

She looked up to find him eyeing her with a mixture of indulgence and resignation. "Help yourself, if you want it," she offered. "I think the heat has done in my appetite."

"More likely you were born without a stomach," he muttered, switching plates with her.

Grinning, Kendall took a sip of her iced tea. Just like old times, she thought. "I'm going to have to learn to cook you larger portions."

"With the way you eat, don't bother. I'll put on a few pounds just by cleaning your plate."

She tossed her crumpled napkin against his bare chest and turned to listen to the weatherman forecast extended hot and humid weather. "Great. A twenty percent chance of scattered thunderstorms. Where's the monsoon when you need one? Even the moon is headed in the wrong direction—full instead of new."

Braden was unperturbed. "Remember, it works both ways; he may be able to see us better, but we'll be able to see him, too."

Kendall accepted that and rose, collecting some of their dirty dishes. When she returned, the news was over. She cocked her head toward the set. "Do you want to watch something else, or should I turn it off?"

"Go ahead and shut it off. I'll entertain myself by following you around."

"In that case, I'll wash and you can dry," she teased.

He didn't mind, but he made all the appropriate protests as he followed her into the kitchen. That made her laugh, which, in turn, made him happy.

"It's so pretty outside this time of day," she murmured, gazing wistfully out the window while she waited for the sink to fill with hot water. "I wish we could go for a walk along the beach."

So much for her ability to stay confined for any length of time. Braden sighed inwardly. What had he originally given her? Three days? Talk about over-estimations—she hadn't lasted three hours!

"Forget it," he muttered.

She shot him a beseeching look. He was smiling tightly, but it didn't begin to reach his eyes. With a sound of exasperation she squeezed some lemon-scented liquid detergent into the water. "It's not as though we'd be unprotected. We have our guns, and Frank's watching, too."

"No."

She wrinkled her nose at him and began washing a glass. "Killjoy," she mumbled. "Well, then, tell me what's new with your mom and dad in Midland?"

Braden relaxed, thinking about his parents. He was an only child, and they'd always been close. Kendall knew a lot about them because he'd always talked about his childhood easily and with affection.

"They're fine," he began. "Getting on in years. I managed to get out there for Christmas."

"Are they still running that little grocery store?"

"No. Would you believe some big development company decided to build a high-rise office building on that property and bought them out? It was like a dream come true. Dad was beginning to worry that he'd have to start hunting for a buyer for the place, and instead one walks through his front door. No more retirement worries for them."

"Oh, I'm so glad. If anyone deserves it, they do."

He told her how excited they'd been when the deal actually went through. "Like a couple of kids," he mused. "They tried to get me to take a loan so I could pay off the rest of my debts, but I turned them down."

"It was a lovely gesture."

"Yeah. They're terrific." He laughed softly. "I finally got them to buy that Air-Stream mobile home they were always talking about getting."

"You're kidding!"

"Nope. They've joined some senior citizens' club and are off seeing the country."

Kendall chuckled delightedly. "Maybe I need to introduce them to Naomi and Fred."

"Not a bad idea." He gave her a funny look. "You know what? They asked about you."

The plate Kendall was washing nearly slipped out of her hands. "Me? Oh, no! You didn't . . ."

"I guess I did." He laughed again, remembering how clever he'd thought he'd been. "You see, I used to write them all the time when I was in Vietnam like some people write in journals or diaries…little things like daily routines, conversations with friends. We've always been close that way. Funny, even after I came home and Maureen and I were married, I still liked to write them these long letters. Can you believe they've kept just about all of them?" His eyes narrowed thoughtfully. "They said the first time I mentioned you was when you gave me that black eye in the volleyball tournament at the annual picnic."

"That was an accident!" she cried.

"Yeah, but it was funny—well, afterward it was," he amended. "Anyway, once we became partners, I guess I wrote about you even more. Now that I look back on things I realize I must have been pretty transparent, but they never let on, except to comment about how much they enjoyed hearing about my work. They didn't say anything when I told them you'd left Houston, either. Then when I went to see them a few months after Maureen died, everything changed. Now that was a sight—each one trying to be discreet and not let the other know what they were up to." His expression softened. "They asked me if I knew where you were and what you were doing, and why I wasn't doing anything about finding out."

"They sound like wonderful people."

"With good taste," he added, with a devilish grin. "I can't wait to show you off to them."

Kendall shook her head, a deep blush flooding her cheeks, but inside her heart was swelling with happiness.

When they finished the dishes, they returned to the living room, and Kendall raised Frank on the radio. They discussed a schedule for the night watch.

"You decide," he told her. "It doesn't matter to me."

"I'll take the first shift," Braden said tugging gently at her ponytail. "Ask him if he wants to take over at three."

Frank agreed, and Kendall signed off, promising to make him breakfast in the morning. When she joined Braden on the couch, he had a troubled look on his face.

"Now what's wrong?"

"Nothing, I suppose. I just don't want Lockwood to find out about Frank. Having him come over will look suspicious."

"I don't think so. Neighbors visit neighbors; if Lockwood is watching that closely, that's all he'll see." Still, she saw his hesitation. "Look at it this way," she teased. "Frank's a worse cook than you are. It's my duty to save you two from yourselves."

Braden slumped back farther into the couch, his teeth clenched against the smile that wanted to come out. "All right," he relented gruffly. "But don't go getting any ideas about going over there with picnic baskets and covered dishes. If he wants to eat, he's got to come here—got it?''

"Got it."

His eyes narrowed suspiciously at her easy acquiescence. "And what are you doing sitting way over there?''

"You put me on rations, remember?''

"Poor baby. Come here." He opened his arms.

She practically threw herself into them, happily curling up against him. When he folded her closer, she sighed with pleasure, loving the feel of him, his strength, and the way his chest hair tickled her as she rubbed her cheek against him.

"Better?''

"Mmpf..." she said, muffling a yawn.

"Don't go to sleep on me," he scolded, laughter rumbling in his chest. "Talk to me. Tell me what you've been doing with yourself all this time? That should fill several hours.''

"Don't be facetious.''

"I'm not. I'll bet if I peeked at your calendar, I'd see it packed with little notes reminding you of all kinds of meetings and activities.''

"I told you, I took a break from that this summer.''

"So you did. Why? You really didn't explain that to me.''

"I haven't really explained it to myself. I just knew I'd come to some crossroads in my life and that it was time to make some changes.''

"Looks like I got here just in time," he murmured somberly. His fingers stroked the soft skin on the inside of her arm.

She tilted back her head to look up at him. In that instant she knew she'd die wanting the image of his face before her. "I still can't believe you're really here," she whispered. "I'm so happy it hurts."

"I know. It's the same for me. I haven't felt this good *and bad* since that first time I kissed you."

He thought back to that one moment when he'd lost control, giving in to the urge that had been slowly driving him crazy. He'd driven her home from a police softball game because her car had been in the shop. It was raining...one of those summer downpours that turned her apartment parking lot into a river. One second he was watching her reach for the door handle, and the next... Something must have snapped in him. Suddenly he was dragging her across the seats of his Mustang and onto his lap, taking her gasping mouth under his with an accuracy born of having dreamt it a hundred times before. For a few exquisite moments they were oblivious to everything, desperately seeking what they knew they couldn't have, taking what they knew couldn't last. Then, that other car pulled into the parking lot, destroying their shadowy oasis. Kendall broke free and ran. Two weeks later she had been gone.

Braden tightened his arms around her until she could barely breathe. He buried his face in the warm curve of her neck and shoulder. "Oh, God, I missed you," he rasped. "So damned much!"

They stayed like that for a small eternity, clinging to each other, offering and taking solace. They learned in that embrace that they were more than would-be lovers, and friends; they were two desperately lonely people who understood each other's pain more clearly than anyone else could and had reached across an invisible divide to battle it together.

"I would think of you at the oddest times," she whispered. "We'd be driving patrol, and there'd be a bunch of college boys tossing a football on a beach, and I'd have to look away."

"The rains hit me worst," he confessed. "I'd be at my desk working on a case and nowhere near a window, and suddenly there'd be a peal of thunder. Then I'd hear it start falling on the roof, and forget it, my mind was finished. I'd make some excuse and go take a long drive until it was time to quit and go home." His chest rose and fell. "If it happened at night, I'd lie in bed or sit by the open window and watch until it was all over."

"I stopped listening to country music."

"I stopped reading your favorite comic strip in the morning paper."

Kendall swallowed with difficulty. "There wasn't one day that passed that I didn't want to pick up the phone and call you, to see how you were, how you were coping with...things."

"It's all right," he murmured, stroking her hair. "The mention of her name doesn't upset me anymore. None of it does, except maybe the incredible waste."

"Would you like to talk about her? You rarely did, you know. We shared so many things, but Maureen and Vietnam were rarely among them."

"Someday...if you'll tell me what it was like for you growing up in those boarding schools, and what you did when the rest of the kids went home for the holidays and you couldn't," he said quietly. When tears filled her eyes, he gently kissed them away. "No, don't cry. I didn't mean to make you cry."

"You've been through so much more than I have...."

He stared down at her soft trembling mouth. "Somehow I doubt that." Slowly he bent, brushing his mouth against hers, unable to resist the temptation. "We'll heal each other. Every day a little more. Okay?"

"Okay," she whispered back shakily.

His breath caught at the longing shimmering in her lovely eyes. "Where's today's paper?" he asked gruffly.

"What?"

"The newspaper." He gently put her back on the other side of the couch. "I thought we'd do the crossword puzzle together...before this gets out of hand."

Kendall took a deep breath and counted to ten. "Okay, crossword puzzle it is," she managed cheerfully. But inside she was miserable, wondering how long they were going to have to go through this torture.

* * *

The telephone rang shortly after ten o'clock. Kendall was making Braden a pot of coffee in the kitchen before turning in herself. She answered it on the second ring. There was a brief silence after she said hello, then a low, unpleasant laugh.

"Hello, beautiful."

It wasn't a voice that would stand out among a hundred other voices, but she knew it was him immediately. She gripped the receiver tightly.

"Hello, Royce." Though they were relying only on the floodlights for light, she could see Braden's expression change as he stood at the living room window. An instant later he was beside her.

"That's good . . . you remember me. A man likes to know he's made an impression."

She ignored that. "Congratulations on making parole. I hope you're not planning on doing anything foolish to break it."

"Is that why Manning is there? Is he worried, too? Did the big man come to warn his little friend . . . protect her from the bad jailbird? Or is he after a little *sugar and spice*?" he taunted.

"You're really getting boring," Kendall snapped.

"We can't have that now, can we? I'll make it up to you later," he promised. "Just tell your boyfriend he's wasting his time: even he can't catch a shadow. Look for me, sweet thing. I'll be right behind you."

"Royce, wait!" Kendall began, but the line went dead. She slowly hung up. She hadn't meant to provoke him, but hearing him talk about her relationship with Braden that way...

Braden cupped her face in his hands and tried to study it in the near-darkness. "I have a vague idea how it went, but tell me, anyway," he said grimly.

She did, ending on a shrug. "He just felt like playing cat and mouse." She took a deep breath and exhaled, expelling the tension that had mounted within her. "I'd better call into the station and have them get started on that paperwork for the tap and trace, after all; then I'll see if I can track down Adam and take him up on his offer. I don't think we can afford any other underestimations of Royce's intentions."

While she was on the phone, Braden radioed Frank to fill him in. When they both finished, Kendall walked over to where he stood, back by the living room window. She could feel the tension in him and lightly began to massage his shoulders.

"When I get my hands on him—" Braden ground out.

"No!" She pulled him around to face her and wrapped her arms around his neck. "Don't talk like that. You don't need to threaten." She pressed her cheek against his hair-roughened chest. "Just hold me. Please...just hold me tight." When he did, she turned her head and pressed her lips to where his heart beat strongest.

He closed his eyes and steeled himself against giving in to what he wanted, yet one hand crept up to cup the back of her head and encourage her. "Let me send

you to Midland,'' he whispered, his voice strained.
"Let me get you out of here.''

"And then what? Braden, he's watching us. Suppose he somehow manages to follow me? That would put your parents in danger, as well.''

She was right. But he was feeling more and more like a time bomb ready to explode. How long could he go on this way?

It cost him, but he moved out of her arms and turned back to the window. "It's getting late, and you have kitchen duty early in the morning,'' he said thickly. "Why don't you go on up to bed and try to get some sleep?''

There would be no peace upstairs for her, alone in her bed. "I'm not tired. Let me stay down here with you. We could—''

"I need some time alone. *Please.*''

There was a note of vulnerability in his abrupt request, but even so Kendall seemed to wilt like a blossom exposed to a sudden frost. "Of course,'' she murmured. "I'm sorry.'' Adding a soft good-night, she left him, her footsteps barely making a sound as she raced up the stairs.

Her hurt cut into him like a knife. What was he doing to her? Who was he kidding? There was no concentrating on Lockwood; not while she was in the same room, the same house. Wanting her, *needing her*, was cutting straight to his soul.

He went to the back window and looked out to where the floodlights illuminated the incoming tide. There was a pulsating rhythm to the dark waves that matched the throbbing in his body. What he wouldn't give to be able to strip and dive into the water's beckoning depths right now and swim until exhaustion obliterated his aching.

Muttering under his breath, he poured himself a cup of coffee and returned to the living room where he began a restless prowl from window to window. Finally he settled in a stiff-backed chair, trying to fight back thoughts of Kendall in bed. He imagined the way she must look, with the sheets riding low, tangled around her long, sleek legs. He imagined her wrapping herself around him the same way, and the lower half of his body jerked spasmodically. Stifling a groan, he closed his eyes. Dawn never seemed farther away.

Six

It was still dark when Kendall awoke. Hot and miserable, she twisted around and glanced at the digital alarm clock on her bedstand. The red luminescent numbers registered 3:47. Wonderful. She wasn't due to get up for another couple of hours, and she was wide-awake.

The house was quiet—quiet and steamy hot. Braden and Frank had changed shifts at three, she recalled, brushing a hand through her hair and then down her feverishly damp body. That meant that Braden was probably asleep by now—if anyone could sleep in this heat. She felt so dehydrated that her throat felt as though she'd swallowed a pailful of beach sand. A glass of water sounded glorious. In fact she was tempted to pour the first one over her head, then let the second one quench her inner thirst.

She slid out of bed and padded to the door, pausing to consider the lavender teddy she was wearing. She'd chosen to wear it instead of a T-shirt because it was a bit cooler. It was also more revealing. Well, so what? she decided. She'd be downstairs and back in a second.

She was halfway down the hallway when a dark, hard form came out of the bathroom and slammed straight into her. Kendall's gasp became a muffled shriek as something wet and icy splashed over her breasts and down her stomach and legs.

"Oh, t-that's c-cold!" she moaned, trying to ease the drenched and clinging satin and lace from her equally drenched skin.

"I thought I'd bring up some ice water," he explained, feeling like the world's biggest klutz. "But I'd already drunk half of it and had to refill the glass. Sorry." He reached into the bathroom for a towel and offered it to her, then, like a masochist who had not yet found his threshold of pain, watched her rub the downy cloth over herself.

"I was going to get something to drink, too," she murmured. Glancing up, she found him staring at her with such intensity that she knew the darkness was providing little protection to her state of undress. "I, um, I thought you'd be asleep by now."

He grunted something and disappeared back into the bathroom, and there was the sound of water running and the remaining ice clinking against the glass.

Then he reappeared. "Here," he said, practically shoving the glass into her hands.

The cool water felt wonderful sliding down her parched throat, and for a moment she gave herself up to that pleasure. She downed the whole thing before handing back the glass. "Thanks," she said breathlessly.

"More?"

The question was barely more than a hoarse whisper. She'd almost missed it because their eyes were locked and telegraphing messages far more profound. Oh God, she thought, feeling her legs turn weak beneath her. I can't bear much more of this.

"No thanks," she said quietly.

He reached back and set the glass on what he hoped was the vanity counter, half expecting to hear it shatter on the tile floor. When he turned back to her, he was unable to stop from staring again at the way the wet satin clung to her. It was no illusion, no fantasy. Every sweet curve was perfection in its most feminine form.

"Do you think I ruined it?" he asked, groping for something to say, desperate to prolong the moment.

"Oh...no." She laughed, a little embarrassed. "It'll dry. No damage done."

No damage except to send all his good intentions to kingdom come. If he thought he could watch her turn around and walk back to her room now, then he was either brain dead or certifiable.

"Take it off," he instructed, his voice a tortured whisper. "It'll dry faster."

Kendall's heart leaped wildly in her breast. Her eyes shot up to his and saw in their depths a wild torment that matched her own. "Are you sure?"

"Never more so of anything in my life."

"Then you take it off."

He closed his eyes briefly. No matter how noble his intentions had been, he'd hurt her, and now, gun-shy, she wasn't about to make the first move. She didn't have to. He'd make everything good for both of them.

Moving a step closer, he took her towel and laid it on the railing. Then he raised his hand to finger the thin satin strap on her right shoulder, feeling its smoothness, and the softer skin beneath it. "I've been a fool," he whispered. "I thought making love would get in the way of things." Needing to temper the rise of his inner urgency, he traced the strap down to the lace bodice. He followed the delicate edge over the gentle swell of her breast and back again. Slowly. Lightly. "I was wrong. Forgive me." With his knuckles, he gently brushed over her nipple, fascinated that the slightest caress could cause her to tremble so. His breath quickening, he cupped her in his palm and let his thumb glide over the tiny bud jutting against the wet satin. "Let me take the hurt away for both of us. Let me love you."

Gently he slid the straps off her shoulders, his breath catching as the lace lingered on the high peaks of her breasts before slipping to her waist. The lightest of touches sent it slithering over her slender hips down to the floor.

His chest rose and fell under the strain of his controlled desire. "Am I dreaming this?" he wondered aloud. "You are incredible." Whispering her name, he drew her slowly toward him, his eyes like molten silver, looking down until the instant their bodies touched. "Yes," he rasped. His great body trembled. "I've dreamed of this . . . wanting you, and being able to give in to that desire."

Kendall splayed and combed her fingers through the dark forest of hair across his chest. "So did I," she whispered. "Even when it was wrong. I couldn't help myself." She explored the contours of his taut muscles, paying deliberate attention to his nipples until they were as firm as her own. Then she laid her parted lips over him and bathed him with the tip of her tongue. Muttering something unintelligible, Braden tangled his hands into her hair.

She lifted her feverish eyes to his. She wanted to drag her body against his to feel the weight of his chest and thighs. She wanted to ignite in him the same fire that was consuming her, but when her lips parted, only the wistful sound of his name broke through.

"I know...I know..." he soothed. Lifting her into his arms, he carried her into his room.

A little moonlight blended with the floodlights and entered through the screened window like a silvery rainbow. Braden eased Kendall down on the bed and watched with fascination as her skin reflected that magical light.

She smiled as he came down beside her. Leaning on one elbow, he traced with his free hand the sleek lines of her body. He tightened his fingers to bring her up against him as he lowered his head.

"Now," he whispered. "Give me that sweet little mouth."

Controlled possession...it was the only name for the way he kissed her. He was so aware of his superior size and strength. Kendall was filled with tenderness for him and his concern, but it was his hunger she craved. She gave herself up to her own, arching closer, tempting him to give her everything.

"Wildcat." His deep voice shook with passion. "You'll make me lose my head."

"I want you to."

Sweet madness. Did she think she could survive it? Would either of them?

He bent his head to her breast. Kendall arched off the bed as he pulled her deeply into his mouth, his hands sliding under her to lift her closer. His tongue and teeth were a sensual assault that drove her to the edge of madness. She cried out, writhing against him, wanting the moment and the exquisite feelings to go on forever.

But Braden had other pleasures to give. He slid his mouth down her body, caressing her slowly. Then, biting her thigh with tender ferocity, he pushed himself off the bed and stripped off his jeans and briefs.

It was Kendall's turn to stare. He was glorious, bronzed and muscular, his body glistening with a fine sheen from the strain of his leashed passion. As he lowered himself onto the bed, his forearms taking the bulk of his weight, she eagerly reached for him and drew his mouth to her parted lips.

"Touch me . . . love me . . ." she entreated.

His hands bit a little roughly into her softer skin as she lured him into a frenzy. "Don't be a dream," he moaned, holding fast. She was scorching him, yet he couldn't get close enough. Her scent went into his blood and drugged him. Everywhere he touched her, she trembled, then arched upward, wanting more.

He raised his head when his fingers slid low into her golden curls and the moist folds of silk beyond, wanting to watch her respond to his sensual assault.

"Braden . . ."

"Let go," he whispered, his own breathing becoming shallow at the tiny erotic sounds she was beginning to make. Then he crushed his mouth down on hers, and his thrusting tongue duplicated the rhythm of his fingers, bringing her higher, closer to the peak.

"Please," she gasped. "Not yet." She reached for him. "Not without you."

"It's been too long," he began. "I won't be able to—" He broke off, clenching his teeth as her gentle fingers feathered over him, dissolving any other thoughts of protest. When she wrapped one smooth leg around his waist and he breached the first centimeters of her warmth, hunger exploded in him. With a groan he pressed her deep into the rumpled sheets and buried himself in her warmth.

The storm broke. Unlike anything they'd ever experienced before, it roared around them and within them, assailing their senses and searing their flesh.

Incredible need and exquisite pleasure set the rhythm that cast them deep into a whirlwind of passion, until reason and consciousness exploded, tearing the breath from their lungs.

Braden slid his hands under her hips and ground her against him as his kiss swallowed their joint cries of ecstasy.

They were still for a long, long time afterward. Even after their breathing stabilized, they seemed reluctant to come out of the tranquil valley they'd settled in.

It was Braden who finally made the first move, rolling over onto his back and taking her with him. He made a long, rumbling, purring sound that reminded Kendall of a big, sated cat.

"Oh, Kendall . . ."

"Hmm?"

"I think I died."

"Bet not."

His newly opened eyes glittered like stars in the darkness. Lying half across his chest, she folded her arms under her chin and gave him an impish smile.

"I love you," she said simply.

With firm but careful hands he dragged her completely over him for a kiss that left them both dazed and breathless.

"Hmm," Kendall sighed, nuzzling his beard roughened cheek. "That was far more eloquent."

"They'll never invent the words I need to describe what I feel for you," he replied huskily. "I wish I could tell you though. You should know just once what it is that you do to me. How you fill every part of me. How I lose track of time, space, everything when you're in the same room with me, until I wonder if I'm not losing my mind." He slowly moved his hands up and down the smooth line of her back, with the subtle beginnings of a new need. It was something else he was learning about himself in relation to her; if he touched her, he had to make love to her. What had he done to make fate so kind to him and grant him that freedom? "I've been blessed," he whispered.

Kendall's heart spilled over with love. She buried her face against his neck. "Braden . . . you make me ache."

Yes. He ached, too, but what a sweet ache. He rolled her beneath him and framed her face within his hands. "Marry me," he demanded urgently. "You didn't say yes when I asked you this morning."

"I don't recall the question coming up." She slid her legs along his, smiling at the way his body tensed. Mischief sparkled in her eyes. "You said you'd spend the rest of your life making me not regret waiting for you. What else do I need?"

Only for a moment did his confidence waver, but he had only to look deeply into the emerald pools of her eyes to regain it. "I was hoping you'd say our children," he said quietly. "Have you thought about it? A baby? Us as a family?"

She managed a tremulous smile. "Yes, I've thought about it. I'd love to have your child. Any preferences?"

For a moment he closed his eyes and silently thanked God for this miracle in his arms. "A boy . . . a girl ... a squadron ... If they're yours, I'll take any-thing and everything."

That sent her into a fit of joyous laughter that didn't end until he kissed her silent. "Mmm ... darling, how many are in a squadron, anyway?"

"I forget. But don't worry. At my age I doubt I could accommodate you ... not if I plan to be around to toss a football to them when they're older." Something flickered in his eyes, and he drew back slightly. "Unless ... oh, brother! Talk about losing it."

"Losing what?"

"Control." He uttered something that could have been a curse or a prayer and bent low to brush his lips in the shallow valley between her breasts. "Sweet-heart, I'm sorry. I didn't stop to think. I mean, I didn't use—"

"It's all right," she assured him quietly. "I'm on the pill. My doctor thought it would be better for me. Nice thought though, huh?"

Braden laced his fingers through hers and drew them to his lips. "Yes, but it's just as well. I'm con-ventional enough to prefer you to have my ring on your finger first."

"That reminds me of something else I want to talk to you about," she mused. "If we got married—"

"When," he corrected firmly.

"*When* we get married, what would you think about my changing my field?"

"If it's the CIA that's wooing you, I'd prefer you tell them that you're not interested."

"I'm serious."

"So am I."

She pinched his side playfully. "I was thinking about something in social services, or maybe juvenile courts. You know, something to do with kids."

"You mean instead of returning an occasional runaway or answering a domestic call, you want to break your heart a dozen times a day." Braden drew in a long breath. He had to admit she'd be good with kids. Her instincts with them were usually right on target, creating a rapport that made them open to her despite the wariness they might feel for the uniform. Still, he'd hate to see her in an environment that could bring back unhappy memories of her own childhood.

"I think I've put most of that behind me," she replied after he'd voiced his concern. "Oh, I know the scars can't go away completely, but I think I can use my experiences in a positive way, and heaven knows some of those poor kids out there could really use the extra attention."

"Then if that's what you want, do it," he said. He knew that when it got right down to it he'd be behind her no matter what she decided to do. He couldn't deny her his support; he doubted if he could deny her much of anything. The vulnerability love caused...

He bent his head low again, needing to reaffirm what he'd just found.

Kendall murmured appreciatively at his blissfully slow caress. She brushed her fingers through his hair and down across his broad shoulders. When he shifted himself between her legs, she knew there would be no more talk of work and jobs tonight.

"You're going to be exhausted in the morning," she whispered, nibbling at the lobe of his ear.

"It'll be worth it." He rolled onto his back and drew her over him. "Even if I turn gray before I'm forty, it'll be worth it."

She sat up, straddling his hips, and lifted her damp hair off her neck. "Complaining already?"

Hunger flared in his eyes as he stared at the tempting picture she made. "Not me," he murmured, sitting up. "Never. Don't move..." His hands were warm on her breasts, and when he added the moist heat of his mouth and tongue, she moaned softly, biting her short nails into his shoulders.

"Braden... I want you now."

"Yes... now..." he said, lifting her over him. His face contorted with fierce pleasure as she took him slowly, completely.

Tiny spasms were already beginning to ricochet through her body, and in her passion she told him of her love. The urgency inside her grew, telegraphing her need to Braden. His deft fingers altered and deepened their ministrations.

"Take me there," he whispered. "Take us there together."

She heard and complied beautifully, wildly, sending them both into climactic fulfillment. Gasping, they clung together, their bodies quaking, glistening, until sanity slowly returned, and there was only the unsteady pounding of their hearts.

"Now I'll be able to sleep," Braden murmured, easing back into the pillows and taking her with him.

Though he was still very much a part of her, he added, "Stay with me."

"Of course."

"Promise?"

Her lips curved into a tender but amused smile. "I think you'd notice if I tried to leave."

His laughter was a rumble echoing deep in his chest. "Beats handcuffs any day," he grinned, tucking her close. He cupped her breast in one big hand and moments later was fast asleep.

Seven

Despite her shortened night, Kendall awoke with the birds. Careful not to rouse Braden, she slipped from his bed and, after a quick shower, dressed in the shorts and top she'd worn the night before. She went downstairs feeling as though she'd downed a half a bottle of vitamin pills.

She set a fresh pot of coffee on to perk and then began mixing together the ingredients for baking-powder biscuits. It was really too hot to use the oven, especially since there was no air conditioner to help cool things off, but this was no time to be practical. She was in the mood to spoil her man, and making him a spectacular breakfast was as good a way as any to start.

Bright eyed, she shook her head in bemusement. Just thinking of him had her breaking out in a silly grin and feeling as if she were blushing all over. She knew she'd better settle down soon because they still had a job to do, but her happiness was like champagne warming her blood, and she wanted to enjoy it a little while longer.

The biscuits had just gone into the oven when she heard the sound of an approaching vehicle. Bruno, punctual as ever, she thought as she glanced at the kitchen clock. She hurried to open the back door.

"Good morning, Fritz," she said to the black-and-tan terrier who raced up the stairs and enthusiastically leaped against her. "You're in a good mood, too, I see."

Bruno brought up the rear, laden down with a shopping bag in one hand and a covered dish in the other. The shopping bag, Kendall surmised, would hold the usual assortment of dishes, toys and food—all Fritz's, naturally.

"Guten Morgen," he greeted, beaming at her from beneath his full, neatly trimmed beard. "I am too early?"

She held the screen door for him and then relieved him of the sack. "Of course not. Besides, it's your schedule that's important at the moment." He assured her that he was fine, and she said, "Well, you look wonderful," noting his light blue suit. Then she indicated the covered dish. "What's this?"

He uncovered another torte and presented it to her with a chef's flourish. "Bruno tries again, *ja?*"

"It's lovely," she cooed, accepting it and putting it on the counter out of Fritz's reach. "You shouldn't have done it—but I'm glad you did. Can you stay and have a slice with a cup of coffee?"

He thanked her but declined. His face grew somber. "Tell me, please, are you okay? This man you spoke of—I vorry for you...."

"Don't," she interrupted kindly. "I'm fine. Fritz will be fine. You just concentrate on having a good time."

When he left, Kendall turned back to Fritz, who sat in the middle of the kitchen floor and watched her expectantly. Kendall grinned, thinking once again that his big chocolate-brown eyes were uncannily similar to his master's. Fritz shook his head impatiently and lifted his paw, wanting the more demonstrative display of affection he knew to expect from her.

She didn't disappoint him. "Hi, buddy," she said with a chuckle, plopping down on the floor and playfully ruffling his wiry fur. "I'm afraid you're going to have to share my attentions with somebody else this visit. Can you handle that like a gentleman? I'd consider it a personal favor because this is a pretty important *somebody*."

The radio clicked a few seconds later, signaling that Frank wanted to talk. Fritz's ears sprang up alertly, and he growled.

"Shh," warned Kendall, springing up to grab the radio off the kitchen table. "Let's keep the barking down to a minimum until after Braden wakes up, okay?" She keyed the radio. "What's up, Frank?"

"Just checking in. Everything all right with Bruno?"

"Yes. He was just dropping off Fritz. Ready for breakfast?"

"I thought you'd never ask."

"Then come on over whenever you're ready. Use the back door." She signed off and went to take the biscuits out of the oven. "You'll have to entertain yourself for a while, my friend," she said, tossing the terrier his favorite rawhide bone from the bag. "I'm going to be busy for the next half hour or so."

Frank looked a bit tired and in need of a shave when she let him in a few minutes later. "Hi, neighbor," he said, holding up a glass measuring cup with an index finger. "Can I borrow a cup of something?"

"Well now, that's effective," Kendall drawled, tongue in cheek. "If only Ginger could see you now. Remind me to put something in it when you leave, in case our friend is an early riser and watching."

"Something edible, I hope. Hey, Fritz! How's things?" he said, leaning over to pat the terrier who'd come over to check him out. "Yeah, take a good sniff. Remember me? I'm one of the good guys."

Kendall went to pour him a cup of coffee while he slid out of his navy blue windbreaker, which had been a necessary cover-up for the revolver clipped to his belt. He hung it over one of the dinette chairs and sat down muffling a yawn.

"Stop that," she said, bringing him his coffee. "You're making me feel guilty for putting you through this."

"Don't. I figure this is good practice for 2:00 a.m. feedings."

She smiled inwardly, wondering if Braden would say something like that when it was their turn. The thought warmed her.

"So—how did the watch go?" she asked.

"Like ninety percent of all of them: minute by slow minute. At 4:00 a.m. two mutts took a stroll down the beach, and that was the highlight of the whole thing." He took a careful sip of the steaming brew and closed his eyes in pleasure. "You make a great cup of coffee, Kendall. If Ginger didn't already own me heart, body and soul, I'd become your slave for a pot of this every morning."

"One of these days that silver tongue of yours is going to get you into trouble, Ortega. How do you want your eggs?"

"Scrambled." He laughed softly. "Ginger still can't face an egg in the morning any other way, and I've acquired a liking for them. Hey, what's this?" he asked, hungrily eyeing the torte she'd set on the table.

Kendall glanced over her shoulder. "A gift from Bruno, as usual. Help yourself."

Not one to require a second invitation, and familiar with Bruno's culinary talents from the treats Kendall had shared with him before, Frank grabbed up the cake knife. "I don't know why you don't weigh two hundred pounds," he murmured, licking his fingers after he'd cut himself a generous slice. "If someone was always bringing me this kind of temptation..."

"I don't have your sweet tooth."

He shrugged good-naturedly. "It's my one vice."

"Give me strength," Kendall moaned.

"Ask Ginger."

"I don't think so."

His dark eyes twinkled with mischief. "Where's Braden?" he asked after a while.

"Still asleep, I hope."

She brought him his breakfast, a platter heaped with sausage links, eggs and biscuits. He had more than a sweet tooth: when it came to food, his appetite was second only to Braden's, despite his leanness. He was one of those lucky few with that type of metabolism, she decided.

"I hope you're going to have something, too?"

"I thought I'd wait and eat with Braden."

"Okay, but get a cup of coffee and keep me company." When she did, he studied her across the small table. "You're happy, aren't you? I mean despite this mess with Lockwood."

"I'm happy."

"Good. I like him, Kendall." He saw her eyes turn over bright and self-consciously looked away. "Well, enough of this sentimentality," he said, clearing his throat. "Let's discuss something sensible, like when you're going to move back to Houston."

The sound of laughter minutes later lifted Braden toward consciousness. He rolled over onto his stomach, burying his face in his pillow, and reached instinctively across the bed.

She was gone, but she had been there. It wasn't a dream like all the other times. Her springlike scent still lingered on the sheets, and his body still felt the satisfaction of holding her close. Smiling, he dragged her pillow beneath him.

God, he felt good. Alive. Whole. The weariness and strain he'd been overwhelmed with lately was gone, shed like an old skin. Last night—or this morning, rather—had been an accident, and unquestionably ill-timed, but there was no way he was going to say he regretted it. And now that she was completely his and he knew how special and necessary their love was, he knew he wouldn't be able to resist her again.

He wanted her now. Just thinking how much made desire surge through him. But she was downstairs, and the next peal of laughter rising from below told him that she wasn't alone. His head cleared swiftly. Who was with her? Frank? No harm in that, but even so he sat up and swung his legs out of bed, and onto something furry.

"What the—"

He leaned over and looked straight into soulful brown eyes. Man and terrier momentarily assessed each other.

"Fritz, I presume? What the hell," he sighed, extending his hand. "Any friend of Kendall's is a friend of mine."

Back downstairs, Kendall wiped tears of mirth from her eyes. "All right, stop the jokes and tell me what you think. Is it a good idea or what?"

Frank laid down his fork and leaned back in his chair, replete. "It's a great idea, but then I'm the guy who's being handed the world on a silver platter. Now if I was your investment counselor, this would be the point where I'd probably start popping antacid tablets."

"Stop! I'm trying to be serious about this." She leaned toward him, her young face eager and as bright as the sunshine warming it.

"Kendall, are you sure?"

"Positive. And I know Braden will be relieved to have it settled."

Frank rubbed his neck. "I have to admit I'd be a fool to turn you down."

"Then don't. Say yes."

He jumped from his chair and swung her from hers, spinning her around and around and shouting, "Yes! Yes! Yes!"

"Frank! Shh—you'll wake Braden."

"Good, since this is worth celebrating. You know you're more than a friend, Kendall. You're an absolute dream!"

Kendall burst into laughter and held on to his shoulders for dear life. The sound of a throat being cleared behind them made them both abruptly turn around.

Braden leaned against the wall, watching them, his arms folded across his chest and with Fritz at his feet. "Good morning. Is this where you convince me that things aren't what they seem?" he murmured dryly.

Kendall rushed over to him. "We woke you up, I'm sorry, darling."

"I'm not," he said gruffly. Ducking, he gave her a swift but branding kiss. "Now, what's all the celebrating about?"

"Wonderful news! I just talked Frank into buying the house. I'll be able to join you in Houston right after I give my two weeks' notice."

His face brightened. It *was* good news. He'd already begun to worry about the separation the house might cause them.

"I'm not sure it's possible, but you look more relieved than I am," Frank said. "Ginger and I have been bandying this problem back and forth for months, trying to figure out what we were going to do. Our apartment is cramped even without the baby that's coming, and I'd hate to waste the rent money on a bigger place, but we haven't exactly saved enough for a decent down payment on a house, either."

"It's decent enough for me," Kendall said. "And with the monthly payments you'll be making, it'll work out fine. Now sit down both of you. Braden, I'll have your breakfast in a second. I see you met Fritz."

Braden glanced over at the terrier, who had gone back to playing with his bone. "He came upstairs to introduce himself."

"He likes to stay in the guest room when he comes to visit," she apologized.

"It's okay. We came to terms."

His words were innocent enough, but there was no mistaking the heated look of possession in his eyes. Kendall felt it down to her bare toes and turned to the stove out of sheer necessity.

Braden's gaze lingered on the curves beneath her loose shorts, and then he forced himself to turn to Frank. "How'd your watch go?"

"Quiet. How long do you think that'll continue?"

"I wish I knew. Maybe I could follow his reasoning if it was based on some kind of sense, but how do you tell which way anger is going to turn? Our best hope at this point is that he's broke and hungry. It would put a damper on any idea he may have about grandstand behavior and it would shut down a lot of his options."

"Unless he's come into some money," suggested Frank. "I'll call into the station and see if there's been any muggings or burglaries in the past twenty-four hours with an assailant who matches his description."

"Good idea."

Frank swallowed the rest of his coffee and rose. "Now if you good people will excuse me, I believe I have more than one important phone call to make, then I'm going to crash for a couple of hours. I'll tell headquarters to call you when they know something. Holler if you need me. Thanks for the breakfast."

"Don't forget this." Kendall handed him back his measuring cup, now filled with her homemade banana-chip cookies. "And here's a casserole you can heat up for lunch or dinner. Tell Ginger I'll call her later. Come on, I'll let you out the front."

When she returned to the kitchen, Braden was at the stove, spatula in hand, poking at his eggs. "Oh, no," she cried, rushing to take over. She whisked the spatula out of his grasp. "Whew...they're just right."

Braden wrapped his arms around her waist. "They're only eggs," he murmured with amusement. "No big deal."

"I had plans to make you the perfect breakfast."

"It is perfect. I'm here with you and we're alone at last—except for our canine friend here, that is. How can you improve on that?" He brushed her hair aside to lay nibbling kisses in the curve of her neck and shoulder.

"Braden..." The plate she'd just picked up wobbled in her hand. "Your breakfast is going to be all over the linoleum if you keep that up."

He laughed huskily. "So will we."

She tilted her head, momentarily giving in to the pleasure of his caresses. It was so easy to forget everything when he touched her.

"I missed you when I woke up," he whispered.

"Duty called." She gave him a loving look over her shoulder. "But I did hate to leave you."

"Congratulations. That's the right answer. You win."

"What do I win?"

"This."

He lowered his head, and his mouth covered hers. Kendall felt the heat and want of his kiss sweep through her body, and she moaned softly. By the time Braden lifted his head, they were both breathing erratically. For several seconds they stared at each other in silent wonder and longing.

"If you don't eat this, it'll get cold."

Mechanically he took the plate. So this is what the real thing felt like, he mused. If he didn't ache so damned much, he'd laugh at himself. He sat down and tried to regroup his lost senses.

Kendall wasn't doing much better. As she poured him a glass of orange juice, she pressed her left hand against her stomach. She felt as though she'd swallowed a dozen Mexican jumping beans. Potent stuff, this thing called love.

"This is great," he said when she sat down beside him. "Listen, this thing about selling the house to Frank—are you sure?"

Kendall frowned. "I really should have talked it over with you first, shouldn't I? I'm sorry. It was a brainstorm, and as usual I got carried away by my own enthusiasm. Sharing decisions is something I'm going to have to get used to."

He reached out to stroke her cheek. "That's not what I meant. The house is yours. The decision whether to sell it or not is yours, as well."

"No," she protested. "That's not the way I want it. Wait. Hear me out," she said as he began to argue. "I don't know how much you still owe—"

"Stop right there." He sat back and shook his head, his expression set. "Do you think I want to start off our marriage by using your money to clean up my mess?"

"I prefer to look at it as a means of solving a problem—a problem that has been keeping us apart far too long already."

"Please don't start using logic on me. It's just not *right*."

His expression was so adorably stubborn that she had to drop her eyes to keep from smiling. "It is when you consider the alternative."

"What alternative?"

"The one that will put you in Houston for the next six months or so and leave me here." Her finger slowly traced the design on a place mat. "Of course, if that's the way you want it.... Frank and Ginger will be disappointed at first, but when I explain to them that it's only a temporary delay, I'm sure they'll understand." She pushed herself away from the table and rose. "I'd better call Frank. Maybe I can get hold of him before he reaches Ginger."

Braden caught her around the waist as she tried to step past him and pulled her backward onto his lap. Sitting eye to eye, he tried his best to glare at her.

"You know damn well he called her the second he got to the house."

"It crossed my mind."

He narrowed his eyes. "And you had no intention of going along with me from the very beginning, did you?"

"I didn't?"

"You little ... you're playing with me."

"Only a bit."

"But you would go through with it. You would stay down here until things were—settled."

She touched the corner of her mouth with her tongue. "If that's the way it has to be."

He dropped his gaze to her lips. Kendall could feel his body tense as he fought some internal battle. In anticipation she parted her lips and absentmindedly toyed with the buttons of his shirt. She played with each one down to his waist and then with the snap of his jeans. It was unfair tactics, but she wasn't interested in fairness at the moment.

Braden's chest heaved. "Make me," he said thickly.

"What?"

"Make me change my mind. Make me realize that I couldn't stand being away from you six more days, let alone six months."

His words seeped through her, causing her body to burn as if she'd just swallowed a whiskey neat. The invitation was clear, and the need behind it even clearer. He was torn between his traditional values and his need to have her with him. All he was certain of was that their love for each other was right.

Kendall's smile held a wisdom as old as time. She slid her arms up around his neck and buried her fingers into his thick, dark hair. Concentrating on his mouth, she leaned close, and even closer. Then she began to kiss him with feathery light strokes of her lips and tongue. Tiny nibbles, teasing his lips until they parted on a ragged sigh. Instead of giving in to what she knew he craved, she moved on across his freshly shaved cheek, the lobe of his ear, the sensitive area within, behind, below. Only when she felt him suck in his breath did she return to his mouth.

The tempo of her caresses increased. She dipped her moist, seductive tongue into his mouth and explored him as thoroughly as he'd explored her the night before, taunting, inviting, until he could bear no more. On a groan of need, he crushed her against him.

She felt so good. So damned good. He restlessly caressed her, molding her body against his, resenting the clothing that separated them but at the same time grateful for them. The way she was touching him was driving him at breakneck speed toward explosion. Grasping at a small remnant of sanity, he tore his mouth free and leaned her back into the curve of his arm. He stroked her with his free hand from knee, to hip, to her ribs. When he covered her breast, his touch gentled, discovering what yesterday he'd only fantasized over. She wore no bra. His thumb teased her, then brushed aside the material that denied him the sight of her.

"Yes... want me," he whispered, watching the helpless reaction of her body. He lowered his head.

Kendall trembled under the heat of his mouth. She raked her hands into his hair, needing to hold him close as spasms of exquisite pleasure shot through her. Again and again she whispered his name.

He raised his head, his eyes burning like wildfire. "I'm going to do that to all of you," he vowed.

"I thought this was my seduction."

Sliding an arm under her knees, he rose and headed for the stairs, both of them for the moment, forgetting Lockwood.

"Next time."

Eight

Kendall stopped at the entrance to her kitchen and bit back an abrupt laugh. Fritz had his grocery sack emptied, the contents scattered across the floor, and he was trying his best to crawl into it himself.

"When I told you to entertain yourself, I didn't have *this* in mind," she declared, standing with her hands on her hips.

Fritz backed out of the bag and gave her a foolish grin. Then he went to the back door and pawed it meaningfully.

"Sure," she muttered, going to unlock the doors for him. "You get to go have more fun while I get to clean up. Stick around, though, okay? If I have to hunt you down while Braden's sleeping, he'll have both our heads."

Locking up behind him, she turned back to the kitchen and shook her head ruefully. It was only mid-morning, and the place looked as if she'd entertained a Cub Scout troop. It was just as well that Braden had drifted back to sleep; she needed to do some industrious cleaning up, and it would be easier to accomplish without having him around as a distraction.

For the next hour she kept herself busy, but as easy as that was, she found her thoughts wandering. There hadn't been any calls from the station, which wasn't a good sign. What was the status on the phone tap and trace? Why hadn't Adam called? *Where was Royce?* Waiting, she decided, was beyond monotonous: it was torture.

When she finished cleaning up, she called Fritz back inside. Then she poured herself a glass of iced tea from the pitcher in the refrigerator. Sipping it slowly, she wandered from window to window, scanning the perimeter. Every piece of brush swaying in the mild breeze earned a second, more intent look, but she doubted Royce was around. Terriers were known to be courageous little trackers, and if he'd been close, Fritz would have found him.

She settled into an armchair by one of the front windows, her thoughts becoming more introspective. She was still annoyed with herself over the way she'd handled that call last night. A rookie could have done better. Women in the police force were supposed to be valued for *depressurizing* potentially dangerous situations...but what had she done? She'd provoked him. Instead of *her* controlling that conversation, *he* had.

She thought about the prison photograph she'd seen of him at the station when she'd read through his file. His small-eyed narrow face had been pale, shadowed from lack of sleep and appetite. He'd still been suffering from the shock of Billy's death, and to Kendall he'd looked like a little old man. She knew there had been no question about the necessity of locking him up, but she had a feeling his tormented soul was in a prison far more severe.

Fritz came over and laid his head in her lap. "Don't look at me like that," she muttered, stroking his head. "You think I'm a bleeding heart, too, don't you? Well, tough. I got into this business to help people, not to overpopulate the prisons."

Giving herself a mental shake, she got up and went to the kitchen. She wasn't going to let herself become overly depressed. There were too many good things happening, and she intended to focus on them!

She decided to call Ginger. Just the thought of the ebullient redhead's laughter brought a smile to her lips.

"I knew it was you!" Ginger said, recognizing her friend's voice. "When I was about to hang up with Frank, I told him that I wanted to call you right away, but he said to wait for your call. How's it going? You sound a little down."

"Cabin fever."

Ginger chuckled. "With you that's serious enough. Oh!"

"*What?* Ginger, what's wrong?" Kendall demanded, instantly alert.

"Mmm...nothing really. Just a nagging case of indigestion."

"Are you sure?"

"*Yes*, mother."

But Kendall wasn't convinced. "What weird cravings have you been stuffing in your face lately?"

"You know me so well. Let's see...it was probably the grilled-cheese-and-sardine sandwiches."

"Yech! I'm sorry I asked."

"Wait till it's your turn."

"Uh-huh. Well, you certainly sound on top of the world otherwise."

"I should hope so," Ginger said with a laugh. "Santa Claus doesn't visit everyone in July, does he?"

"I assume that means you'll take the house?"

"When can I come help you pack?"

Kendall grinned at the receiver. "Thanks a lot, friend. The least you can do is tell me that you'll miss me. Maybe a few crocodile tears would be appreciated."

"Oh, hon, you know I'm going to do that, but right now I'm too happy for you." Ginger's light soprano dropped a full octave. "And I'm *dying* to know all the sizzling details about you-know-who. Frank says he's a hunk."

"Frank said *that*?"

"Well, with Frank you have to read between the lines," Ginger amended, dismissing the technicality. "But I'm right, aren't I?"

"Oh, yes. He's really something."

"My, my...and when do I get to meet him?"

"After I have a ring on my finger," teased Kendall.

Her friend's laughter took awhile to subside. "Bless you. You really know how to make a pregnant lady's day. Lately I swear the only thing giving me the eye are the watermelons in the grocery store. But let's not get off the subject—namely you. Do you mean to tell me that all this time I've been trying to match you up with somebody, pulling out my hair when nothing seems to click, and you—you sly thing—had someone all along?"

"No, of course not. Braden and I haven't seen each other since I left Houston." Kendall fingered the coiled receiver cord. "It's a long story. I guess Frank told you that we used to be partners?"

"That's about all he could figure out—and the fact that you two seemed nuts about each other. Is he the reason you left Houston in the first place?"

"Yeah. I had to once we realized that we felt more for each other than friendship. He was married, Ginger."

Her friend whistled softly. "Now I get it. God, that must have been awful for both of you. What I wouldn't give to drag you over here for a good old gossip session. I have a feeling that you're leaving out all the good parts."

"Maybe you should have been a detective," replied Kendall fondly.

"Well, answer me this, and I'll let you off the hook for now; if you two are getting married, what's happened to his wife?"

"She died. She'd been very sick."

"Oh." Ginger was silent a moment. "It sounds like you two have really been through the wringer. But it's all turned out for the best. I'm really happy for you both."

"Thanks, but do you know what still gets to me?" Kendall sighed wistfully. "If it wasn't for Lockwood's threat, Braden admitted he might never have come after me. He has this ridiculous idea about not being good enough for me."

"Men . . . don't you just love them? That's why fate steps in to set things straight," philosophized Ginger airily. "If our guys kept us up on that pedestal they're always placing us on, civilization would have dried up a long time ago."

Kendall moaned. "Leave it to you to simplify things. There's something else I wanted to tell you. I really feel uncomfortable about Frank getting involved with this—"

"Not another word," her friend warned. "You're like family to us. If Frank hadn't volunteered, I would have drafted him."

"You're one in a million."

"So are you."

Kendall ended the call shortly afterward. She wanted to call the station and see what the latest developments were, if any.

About an hour later Braden came downstairs and found her bent over a map of the city at the kitchen table. He leaned over her, gently tugging at her ponytail, and demanded a kiss.

"How was your nap?" she asked, smiling into his eyes.

"Great, except that my favorite pillow keeps deserting me. What's all this?" he asked, glancing at the notepad she was working from and the markings she was making on the map.

"Probably nothing more than a waste of time, but I called the station and got the list of reports filed in the past two days—remember, like Frank mentioned? They weren't able to match Royce with anything in the cases where there were witnesses, so I'm laying it all out and then trying to mark in the cheaper motels in the area, abandoned houses and buildings to see whether it would be feasible for him to have been there." She straightened and rubbed a kink out of her neck. "As I said, it's probably a waste, but I've got to do something before I go stark raving mad."

"Come here," he said, drawing her into his arms. He folded her close and rocked her gently. He knew what this was like for her. Staying shut inside went as much against her nature as trying to capture a wild creature and trying to pen it. She was meant for sunshine and space and activity, and the easiest way to break her spirit was to deny it to her. "You're doing great, and your idea is a good one. Let me dig up a sandwich or something, and you can show me what you've got so far."

"Let me," she said, eager for the smallest task. "You must be starved by now. You hardly ate breakfast."

"Mildly ravenous," he agreed.

While she prepared for him a double-decker ham and cheese sandwich, she filled him in on what else was going on downtown. "Oh, and they've got the consents for the tap and trace. As usual, the phone company gave them a harder time than the judge."

"Where are they going to set up the tap box?"

"Here. Adam's bringing it over in a little while." She saw Braden's brows draw together and added hurriedly, "They wanted to keep things looking normal. Milk, iced tea or orange soda?"

"Orange soda." He smiled, remembering it was her favorite.

She took it out, popped the top and pushed it into his hands along with his sandwich plate. "To no one else would I bequeath my *last* can of orange."

"Must be love," he agreed, taking a seat.

While he ate, she showed him her progress and continued filling in data. They exchanged ideas with the easiness of two people who knew the inner workings of the other's mind.

"What do you think?" he asked at last, pushing his empty plate away.

Kendall studied the map a moment longer. "I don't think he was involved with any of these. And unless he came from Houston with money in his pocket, I'd go on to agree he's hungry, tired and strung out."

Braden started to comment but was interrupted by the phone. "I'll get it."

It was Captain Fielder from Houston, so Kendall busied herself with folding up her map and rinsing off the dishes. She didn't expect him to be able to add anything new to their dilemma, but she found it touching that he was checking on them.

"He sends you this," Braden said, creeping up behind her a few minutes later to kiss her tenderly on the cheek.

A soft rush of color flooded her cheeks. "How is he?"

"A little worried, though you couldn't get him to admit it."

She nodded. "Another tough ex-marine, like somebody else I know." The telephone rang again, and she and Braden exchanged wary looks. "My turn," she murmured.

It was Ginger—or at least she thought it was Ginger. She was crying and nearly hysterical. "Please," Kendall begged her. "Slow down. Take a deep breath and tell me what's wrong."

"The baby...Kendall, call Frank...*please*. I forgot to get his n-number, and...it's too soon!"

Kendall quickly put her hand over the mouthpiece. "Raise Frank and tell him he's got to get home fast," she said to Braden. "I think Ginger's gone into premature labor."

Then she went back to Ginger, assuring her that everything was under control. "No, I won't hang up," she promised. "I'll stay on the line with you until Frank gets to you. Have you called for an ambulance?...That's good. Okay, here's what we're going to do..."

Confidently, quietly, she coached Ginger to start the breathing techniques they teach in natural childbirth classes. Though inside she was screaming at the injustice of it all, she brought Ginger back down from her hysteria so that they could almost converse normally between exercises. Frank and the medics burst through the door simultaneously, and Kendall finally hung up, knowing the rest was in someone else's hands.

Braden, grim-faced, was beside her immediately to take her in his arms. "It's not fair! It's not fair!" she whispered hoarsely through helpless tears.

"Don't," he soothed. "Everything will be fine. You have to believe that. Lots of babies are born premature." He brushed away her bangs and delivered several soft kisses across her warm brow. "You did a magnificent job there, lady. Where'd you learn that breathing stuff?"

"I took a course with a young girl I'd brought into one of the crisis centers."

She left it at that, and Braden didn't push it. He knew her well enough to know that the story was a grim one and that the girl had become one of Kendall's lost sheep.

"Did Frank take one of those courses?" he asked thoughtfully.

Despite everything Kendall managed a low laugh. "Are you kidding? By the fourth session he and the instructor were arguing over another technique he'd picked up in a library book. Poor Ginger was mortified." She shook her head. "The man's obsessed."

Maybe, Braden conceded, but he could understand that kind of obsession. He had only to look down at the small woman in his arms . . .

"I really should go next door and check the house," she said, forcing herself to push aside the dark thoughts that tried to dominate her mind. "The way Frank's truck tore out of here...I need to at least check that he locked the doors. I spoke to Ginger a little more than an hour ago. She had indigestion. What could have happened?"

"Come on." Braden turned her into the living room and up the stairs. "Let's get some shoes on, and I'll walk you over."

When they met back downstairs, he was also wearing a black short-sleeved shirt and his shoulder holster. As he checked his clip, Kendall retrieved her revolver from the kitchen table.

"Not very subtle, are we?" she murmured, tucking it into her waistband.

He held the front door open for her. "Somehow I don't think it matters much."

The heat was oppressive and the glare blinding, but Kendall felt better once she was outside. She took deep breaths of the rich sea air and smiled tolerantly as Fritz energetically raced around them. She knew exactly how he felt. She wouldn't mind a little sprint to burn off some excess energy herself.

At the Cheeseys' she went in alone. Frank had locked the front door, and she used her extra key to get in. The house was appealingly cool and dark, reminding her once again of what they were having to put up with at her place—as if she needed reminding. Now that Frank was no longer around, she turned up the temperature control and quickly did a check of the rest of the house. Except for an overturned chair that he must have tripped over in his race out the door, everything seemed fine. She reported as much to Braden when she rejoined him outside.

"You know we'll have to phone this in."

"Yes." She made a furrow in the sand with the toe of her tennis sneaker. "But—what if we didn't?"

"Come again?"

"What if we both went away? Together. I could phone the station and tell them that's what we'd decided to do. It would spare them from having to find someone to replace Frank. Simpson would approve. We could find someplace quiet, safe, and eventually Royce would give up."

"He's not going to give up. How long are you willing to let this hang over our heads?"

Kendall's fingers curled into her palms. His quiet words were a challenge she couldn't turn from. How long, indeed? Would it be worth risking a few days' or a week's peace of mind for a lifetime of living with the threat of terror?

"Don't try to take the blame for Ginger," he continued gently. "You don't know that it wouldn't have happened, no matter where Frank had been. The important thing is that he's with her now."

"You're reading my mind again," she complained.

"It's a beautiful mind. Kind. Generous." He slipped his hand to cup the back of her neck and bent low to give her a brief but tender kiss. "Nothing is going to happen to us as long as we stick together. Believe that."

"I'm trying. But I want this over. I want this over so badly."

His fingers contracted lightly. "Me, too."

She gave him a tremulous smile, then glanced over his shoulder. "Here comes Adam. We'd better get back."

They walked briskly toward the silver Mercedes, following Fritz, who was charging to investigate. Adam got out of the car, looking as if he'd just come from the golf course. He wore a grass-green polo shirt and slacks in a more pastel shade. It contrasted attractively with his dark tan and sun-bleached hair.

"Hello!" He bent to kiss her cheek, adding in a stage whisper, "What the hell are you doing out?"

"We had to check things next door. I'll explain inside." She gave the gift-wrapped box he was holding a quizzical look. "Is it my birthday again?"

"Don't get cute," he said, handing it to her. "I thought I was being very clever."

"You are. Shake hands with Braden, and let's go in."

The two men exchanged cool, appraising glances behind her back. Adam, a veteran of more battles of diplomacy, extended his hand, with a hint of challenge in his pale blue eyes.

"This doesn't have to be binding," he murmured.

"It would please her if it was." Braden took it. "Thanks for coming...and for your help."

"How many IOUs did you have to give out for this?" Kendall asked when they were all inside. She set the package containing the tap box on the coffee table, along with her gun.

"Let's just say I don't expect to win another golf game this season." He shrugged, letting her know he considered it insignificant. "How are things here?"

"They could be better." She told him about Ginger and Frank.

"That's rough," he murmured sympathetically. "What about Lockwood?"

"Nothing since I called you last night."

"He sounds like a real sweetheart."

Kendall wearily rubbed the back of her hand across her brow. "Well, a pretty mixed-up one, anyway."

Adam and Braden exchanged surreptitious glances. "I'm going to call the station for you and report the situation with Frank," Braden said, squeezing her shoulder lightly.

"Okay, thanks."

Adam considered her for a moment in silence. "I know you're used to being under pressure," he began with quiet concern. "But you look tired, Kendall."

"I'm a little worried about Ginger. I'll be fine, though." She gestured toward the kitchen. "Let me get you something."

"Thanks, but I really have to go."

Braden heard the Mercedes driving away a few minutes later as he hung up the phone. He went into the living room and picked up the gift-wrapped box, a wry smile tugging at his mouth. He had to admit it beat bringing it in with an attaché case, as he'd expected the lawyer to do. As he began to tear off the wrapping, he heard Kendall calling frantically for the dog. In the same instant he saw her gun on the coffee table.

He shot out the door in time to see her racing down the driveway and disappear around a dune. Then came a scream and the gut-wrenching sound of tires screeching to a halt.

"Kendall!"

He was off the porch and running before the dread in that cry echoed back in his own ears. He heard a truck shift gears and drive off. His world went black. Tearing around the same dune, he braked, barely in time to keep from colliding head-on into her. White-faced, she stared at him while Fritz, in her arms, licked happily at her chin.

"Oh, God..."

"I—he ran after a cat," she stammered. "It's the one thing he hates. Cats."

Braden swallowed, trying to get air back into his lungs. The look he gave her was murderous. "I thought—I heard— *Damn it*, I thought that truck hit you!"

"Not quite. I mean he was in more danger," she said, hugging the terrier.

He stared at her in disbelief. "Are you crazy! You risked your life for a *dog*?"

"Not *a* dog. Fritz." She stepped around him and started up the drive. "And there's no need to be sarcastic." Halfway to the house she put Fritz down, and he took off merrily toward the porch. "I know I took a risk," she added.

"More than one, lady. Your gun's inside, or haven't you noticed?"

"Oh, for... I didn't plan this to happen!"

"Great. That'll look terrific on your headstone," he shot back. Suddenly he spun her around and, grabbing her by the arms, shook her violently. "You little idiot, I love you! I've waited years to be able to say that to you. Do you think I'm going to stand around and watch you test fate?" For a moment he just stared at her. With her hair windblown and her cheeks now suffused with color, he wondered if she'd ever looked more lovely. Did she know how precious she was to him? A low groan broke from him as he hauled her into his arms.

Blindly he sought her lips. All the fear and anger he was feeling went into that kiss, as if he were trying to purge them out of himself. He plunged his tongue deeply into her mouth in near-assault.

Kendall's gasp ended in a whimper. She clutched at his shoulders, feeling the vital strength of him and spasmodically flexed her fingers. Any thought of resisting was fleeting, for before she could draw another sweet breath, his possession gentled into seduction, and against that she had no resistance.

When Braden raised his head, they were both breathing in shallow gasps. His burning gaze swept over her uptilted face, taking in her dreamy expression. Without a word he took her hand, drew her up to the porch, and then swept her and the terrier inside.

"What am I going to do with you?" he muttered, pressing her back against the bolted door. "I start out by reading you the riot act and end up by making love to you."

"You don't hear me complaining, do you?"

Braden bent and nipped lightly at her bare shoulder and neck. "The problem is you should be listening to me, and you don't."

"If they're always like that, I like your punishments better," she murmured, tipping back her head and smiling invitingly. Then she saw the remaining shadows of torment in his eyes. She bit her lip. "I'm sorry," she whispered, wrapping her arms around his neck. "But only for leaving my gun—not for going after the dog."

"Kendall—"

"You just kissed me out there for all the world to see. Tell me honestly if you were consciously thinking at that moment like a cop, or even worrying about Royce Lockwood? What I'm trying to say is, we all do things sometimes that may not be the wisest, but at the moment—"

"It's all we can do."

"Exactly."

He hung his head in exasperation. "I told you I can't stand it when you get logical on me."

"Now who is being difficult?" she chided tenderly.

He was silent for a long moment, fighting some inner demon, finally expelling his breath with a heavy sigh. "Okay," he relented. "The subject's closed."

"Good."

"For this time."

"Of course." She went on tiptoe and kissed him on the chin. "I'm reasonable. Now why don't you hook up that box while I go strangle the dog."

Nine

What do you mean our backup can't get here until after ten?...Yes, I know this is an unusual situation...I understand that, too...No, there hasn't been further contact with the suspect." Kendall intercepted Braden's sympathetic look and rolled her eyes. "No, I don't want a regular patrol car cruising the area in the meantime; that would be defeating the purpose, wouldn't it?..."

When Kendall hung up the telephone a minute later, she took a second to close her eyes and shake her head, as if to clear it. "What was I saying the other day about being swamped with protection? Suddenly I feel more like the lost patrol."

"Don't let it get to you," Braden soothed. "It'll be okay. Besides, they're right; so far everything has been quiet."

He watched her go to the oven to check on her casserole. Desire ignited helplessly. She'd taken a shower earlier in the afternoon, and with every movement she made, her hair swung around her face like a veil of gold silk. Wearing a yellow-and-white striped tank top and yellow shorts, she reminded him more of a bright little bird than a streetwise lady cop. A harassed lady cop, he amended with commiseration.

"It's going to be another ten minutes or so," she estimated, frowning into the oven window. Her fingers tapped an impatient code on the countertop. "Do you want another glass of iced tea?"

"You just refilled it," he reminded her, going back to flipping through her high-school yearbook.

"Oh. Right."

He sighed and set it on the table. "Stop worrying."

"How can I? It's been hours," she fretted. "This isn't like Frank. He should have called by now."

"Maybe there's nothing to report."

"Well, he could have reported *that*!"

Braden smiled. "Then try believing in that old adage about there being good news in no news."

Maybe, she thought. Didn't they say that first babies often took longer? She glanced at the clock again and winced. Poor Ginger. She went back to pacing. She checked the view from the living room windows and then returned to the kitchen. "It's going to rain," she murmured, peering out the back window. "The clouds are building up toward the southwest."

"Good," he replied absently. "Maybe it'll keep the natives indoors tonight."

She glanced over her shoulder and grimaced. Where in the world had he found that book? She thought she'd managed to bury it somewhere. "Will you put that thing away?" she pleaded.

"Why? I'm enjoying this. Hey—you never told me that you were the school mascot!" He chuckled, lifting the book closer. "Well, will you look at that? How did they pin that thing to the back of your leotard?"

Kendall shot across the room, snatching the book from his hands and quickly tossed it onto the top shelf of the living room closet. So much for her senior year—her first and only year in a coed high school.

Braden caught her wrist as she came back into the kitchen and pulled her onto his lap. "Don't be embarrassed," he said, stroking her cheek. "Everybody feels funny about having someone else see their yearbook. Besides, I thought you looked adorable in that outfit."

"Adorable! I wanted to be a cheerleader and look *sexy*."

"At *seventeen*?" She gave him a sidelong look, and he grinned sheepishly.

"I was desperate to fit in, but how could I? All the girls had boyfriends, dates and breasts! Me? I was small, flat-chested, and cute. Oh, how I learned to loathe the word *cute*. I might as well have been somebody's toy poodle. Being the school mascot perfectly summarized my existence. I was everybody's pet, and no one thought of me as a *person*."

Braden's heart ached. So much love to give, he thought, and no one to give it to. He brushed her hair behind her ear and kissed her brow softly. "I'd like to think nature was trying to keep you a secret for me to find," he whispered. His other hand slid up over her ribs and stroked her gently. "See? Breasts and everything."

"Idiot," she giggled, burying her face in his shoulder.

"I still think it's fun to know that my nickname for you was right on target."

She groaned theatrically. "Do you know you were the first person that I didn't mind calling me that? Before it made me want to take a swing at somebody. But you—" She wriggled on his lap, snuggling closer against him.

Heat shot into his loins, and he drew a quick breath. "Yeah?" he muttered, seeking her mouth. "Me what?"

But before she could answer, the phone rang. She leaped off his lap with more enthusiasm than he thought appropriate.

"Hello?...Frank!" She listened briefly and then let out a whoop of delight. "I'm an aunt!" she cried to Braden.

Braden grinned despite himself, enjoying her exploding enthusiasm and the way she began to barrage Frank with questions. But a few minutes later the questions turned into counterdirectives, and from the one-sided conversation he could pretty much tell what was going on. He got up and took the phone from her.

"Frank—congratulations, buddy!...Yeah, I figured that out...Are you sure?...No, that's not too late. You've still got the key, right...Then we'll see you later. Give Ginger a kiss for us."

He hung up and quickly pressed his fingertips against Kendall's mouth before she could protest. "It's the way he wants it."

"But he should stay with Ginger."

"They won't let him stay all night."

"Then he should go home and rest."

"Sweetheart, you heard him. He was in the delivery room with her. He's so keyed-up, it'll take hours for him to wind down again."

"Oh, all right."

He hugged her briefly. "Now go get that casserole out of the oven before it turns to rock, and I'll phone in and cancel the other backup." But when she turned away, he stopped her. "Wait a minute, Auntie Kendall. Aren't you going to fill me in on what the stork brought you? Niece or nephew?"

Her face lit up with a wide grin. "A niece. Imagine that . . . a little girl."

Being together already set a glow to Braden and Kendall's shared moments, but relief and happiness for the Ortegas made dinner particularly special that night. They opted to eat at the coffee table again, but this time left off the TV. They were too busy talking to have paid attention to the news, anyway. Kendall added a candle to the table for a touch of festivity and romance, and as the evening sun rapidly sank on the horizon, it became a bridge over which their gazes drifted and held.

"Someday soon I want to do this again," murmured Braden, touching his iced tea glass to hers. "But with wine and a fur rug, and you in something like you wore last night."

Enchanted by his mellow voice as much as his words, her eyes grew dark. "And what will you be wearing?" she breathed.

"Not a damned thing."

"I'll be a little overdressed, won't I?"

"Not for long."

Her body turned to liquid at the thought. A small moan broke from her lips. "Braden...you don't play fair."

"What makes you think I'm playing?"

"I can't eat when you look at me like that, and my body is demanding food."

"You're right. Eat," he said gently. "I won't have you getting ill. I'll save my fantasies for when you can afford to give me your undivided attention. This is really good," he added, turning back to his own plate.

Gratefully she grabbed at the change of topic. "Was Maureen a good cook?"

"Oh, Lord." Abruptly he burst into laughter. "No. She was the first person I'd ever met who made grilled cheese sandwiches without removing the cellophane wrappings on the individual slices. Stoves shuddered when she walked through the appliance section in a department store. While I was in Nam, the fire department visited the apartment twice to put out grease fires." He shook his head, his expression rueful. "Her discovery of TV dinners probably saved my life."

Kendall laughed, as well. Then she reached across and touched his hand. "I'm glad that there are memories you shared that you can still smile over," she said sincerely. "I'm glad the bad times didn't erase them."

He searched her sunny face, her bright green eyes that were brimming with adoration, and felt his own love swell in his chest. Dear God, how did she do it? he wondered. How did she accept so easily, remaining tolerant to the very things that have kept her from her own happiness?

He was still pondering that a couple of hours later as she lay asleep on the couch. He'd decided that Adam was right: he'd overheard Adam tell her that she look tired, so after they'd cleaned up the dinner dishes, he'd insisted that she lie down.

He turned from the window to look at her, as he had been doing every few minutes. She was so lovely, lying there in the darkness, her hair spilling over the pillow like spun moonbeams, her skin pale, almost glowing. Against her cheeks her long lashes looked like russet velvet. Every shallow breath she took pronounced the gentle swell of her breasts.

He watched her possessively as he crossed the room and slipped to his knees beside her. He knew rousing her would be nothing short of selfish, knew he should let her sleep, but the need to touch, to reaffirm, was too strong.

Kendall rose from the languorous nest of a deep sleep to another dream of subtle sensations. She felt as though a warm tide was flowing over her body, and she stretched lazily, relishing the delicious feeling.

"Wake up, little cat," Braden whispered against her lips.

Emerald green opened to silver...and melted. "Hello...I've just had the most erotic dream." Her right hand lifted to stroke the hard muscles of his cheek. He turned and planted a kiss in her palm.

"I'm having one now."

The distant rumble of thunder drifted through the windows. Kendall listened, then her mouth curved invitingly.

"That was in my dream. I've always wanted to make love during a storm."

They'd almost started to—once. He groaned softly and slid his mouth to her wrist. He found her scent and followed it to the crook of her elbow, to her shoulder, her throat. "I want you," he whispered against her fluttering pulse. As his hands drifted over her he rediscovered the silk of her skin. She was so slender, so fragile, that just the feel of her made him ache. Her touch made him shudder. In desperation he sought her mouth.

There was no air where he was taking her, yet Kendall went, wrapping herself around him because she had no choice.

His touch became deliberate. He sought her breasts, burying his face between them, absorbing their warmth and the butterfly beat of her heart. His feverish mouth brushed over each gentle peak, adding to her warmth and then wetting her with his tongue.

"You're torturing me," she whispered, arching off the couch.

He shifted his body over hers, locking their hips
with a fierce, primitive need and rocking against her.
He clenched his teeth against the exquisite agony.
"Listen to the wind," he coaxed against her ear.
"Come to me in that sweet, wild way."

Kendall's blood caught fire. His name was a
breathless entreaty as she sought and found his mouth,
ending in a whimper as he crushed it down on hers.
She was born for this man, this moment, and gave
herself up to it with pleasure.

Frenzy overcame them. Fingers fumbled against
fingers, buttons and cloth. Half dazed, she felt cooler
air rush over her bare skin and smiled. She loved it—
the feeling, the freedom—but most of all she loved the
way he was looking at her. No man had ever made her
feel more like a woman. She raised her arms and
combed her fingers through her hair, drawing his attention to the impudent thrust of her swollen breasts.

"Silk and cream..." he whispered, lowering his
mouth to her.

He rushed her close to the first peak, but when her
trembling fingers reached for the snap of his jeans, he
shifted away to finish undressing her. His mouth followed, eager to give her as much as he could before he
lost his head completely. Then that moment came
when he finally stood to strip off his jeans and saw her
eyes move down his body with wild hunger.

Muttering an oath, he slid down over her and into
her. His mouth muffled her gasp and drank the moan
that followed. And then there was only ecstasy and
their race to leap from its pinnacle.

Bright light flashed behind Kendall's closed lids. Reluctantly she lifted them. The storm was close now, and the thunder angry. She sighed blissfully, not caring. Her fingers stroked Braden's back.

"Was I too rough?" he murmured against her neck.

"No." She grinned. "Was I?"

His chest shook slightly. "Yeah. I'm beat." He muffled a yawn. "I think I'd better go upstairs and wake myself up with a cold shower."

"Don't you have that a little backward?"

"Wise guy." He kissed her hard and pushed himself off the couch. "I want to be awake when Frank gets here. Think you can hold down the fort for a few minutes?" He collected his clothes and gun and headed up the stairs.

"Sure." She reached for her own clothes just as a great flash of lightning illuminated the room. The thunder that followed was almost deafening. "Braden? Where's Fritz?"

"Outside. Nature called."

"When?"

"Just before I woke you," he replied, giving her a wink before he disappeared into the bathroom. A moment later the shower started.

Poor Fritz, thought Kendall. He disliked lightning almost as much as she did. It was a wonder that he wasn't tearing the back door down.

She no more than got her tennis shoes tied when lightning and thunder seemed to hit simultaneously, and the electricity went out. Momentarily startled, she grabbed for her gun.

Upstairs Braden slammed the shower door open. "Kendall?" he shouted.

"It's okay. I think lightning must have struck a terminal or something. Don't worry. It'll probably be back on in a few minutes."

"You sure?"

"Happens all the time out here."

She tucked her gun into her shorts and went to call Fritz. Never a dull moment, she sighed to herself.

The wind was blowing fiercely, and she held tightly to the screen door to keep it from flying back against the house. She had to squint against the sand that pelted her, but worse than the sand, there was no sign of the terrier. She called for him, her voice all but drowned out in the howling wind.

Great. Now what was he up to? She called him again. It would be just like him to go home and try to get in there, she thought, looking toward Bruno's. With each flash of lightning she tried to look for a sign of movement, an image that resembled his.

Serve him right if she let him stay out during this. This was the second time today for him to give her trouble, and that was two times more than her nerves needed at this point.

Then guilt replaced her annoyance, and worry. Could he have gone into the road again? Was he at this moment lying out there in the darkness, maybe bleeding, or his little body broken. She shook her head, pushing away the images that flashed in her mind. She called for him again, this time as loudly as she could.

A heartrending howl drifted back at her, but the way the wind was blowing, she wasn't sure where it was coming from. She walked out onto the deck to the railing and, cupping her hands around her mouth, tried once more.

This time he barked and yelped. She could almost make out the entreaty in it, and she was sure it was coming from Bruno's house.

Don't tell me he's gotten himself stuck in his pen, she thought dismally, remembering the wire fencing behind the house where Bruno often put him when he worked. It had a wooden door with an extremely flexible hinge and a latch that would automatically lock if slammed. With this wind that could happen easily.

"Damn—damn—damn!" she whispered. Of all the times for this to happen. If she went to get him, Braden would have her head—especially after what happened today. But how could she leave Fritz out there? Not only was he her responsibility, but she dreaded to think how upset Bruno would be if anything happened to his dog.

She made her decision as the first drops of rain began to fall in heavy pellets. If she made a run for it, she might make it there and back before she got too wet.

"North," she muttered with resignation, "this is not the brightest thing you've ever done." Adjusting the gun in her waistband, she took off running.

Bruno's house was only a few hundred yards from her own, but to Kendall it felt like a mile—especially when halfway there the skies opened up to a torrential rain. Silently she called herself every version of a fool. No, she was never going to explain this to Braden. Of course, the way the lightning was playing dive-bomber around her, she might never get around to even trying.

She raced around to the back of Bruno's house, and sure enough, there was Fritz, nicely locked up, looking a lot like she felt, she supposed. When he saw her, he gave a happy yelp in greeting and leaped against the fence.

"Thanks. Nice to see you, too," she sputtered, brushing soaked hair and water from her face. "Come on. I have a feeling we're about to test the theory about you being man's best friend."

She was reaching for the latch when she was abruptly yanked back. Then a knife was pressed sharply against her side.

"*Freeze*...don't even think of moving, or I'll do much more with this than scratch your pretty skin," Royce Lockwood hissed against her ear. His left hand slid around her waist, and he removed her gun. "All right. Slowly—take a step back from the gate and turn around. *Slowly*. And keep your hands up," he ordered, stepping back from her.

Kendall closed her eyes briefly in self-disgust. Then, taking a deep breath to temper her surging adrenaline and pounding heart, she did as he instructed.

"Welcome to my party," he drawled, seemingly pleased with himself.

"Hello, Royce."

Her eyes swept over him, lingering on the way he had her revolver pointed at her. Better not look at it, she told herself. Look at his eyes. Maintain eye contact... and wait for the right moment to make your move.

He stood a safe six feet or so away from her, seemingly oblivious to the fury going on around him. Only his eyes were slightly narrowed against the onslaught of driving rain. He was thinner than she remembered him to be, almost gaunt, with his dirty T-shirt and jeans all but hanging off him. But she wasn't about to underestimate what he was capable of. He might have had a rough few days, but when he'd come up behind her, she'd sensed a crafty agility in him that was not to be dismissed. The picture hadn't lied; prison had aged him. The short prison-regulation haircut didn't help, though she didn't see any gray in the dark brown bristles. He needed a shave, too.

"Taking inventory?" he sneered. "Me, too." His gaze drifted over her, lingering in places where her clothing was plastered most. "I think I like you better out of uniform, Officer North. A lot better."

Kendall forced herself to ignore that and the temper that rose in her. What was most important at this point was not her vanity, but buying time.

"That's a pretty slick maneuver you pulled," she said quietly. "What did you do, follow me over here?"

"You think I left this to chance?" he scoffed. "I knew you'd both underestimate me. I planned it all. You thought you two were so clever trying to hide in that house, thinking I'd have to come in to get you."

"Isn't that what you planned? Isn't that why you sabotaged my air conditioner?"

He shrugged. "I figured it couldn't hurt...just in case, you know? Besides, I wanted to keep you on your toes, wondering what I was going to do next. But I knew you'd come out eventually. Like today with the dog. Somebody almost did half my job for me, didn't they?" He saw the startled flicker in her eyes and laughed softly. "Yeah, I was there. You sure do make a fool of yourself over this mutt, lady."

"So people keep telling me," she acknowledged ruefully. "Did you lock him in there?" she added, nodding with her head.

"He was pretty accommodating. All I had to do was throw some food scraps in there and shut the door behind him."

Kendall chanced a glance at Fritz over her shoulder.

"Don't move!" Lockwood snapped. "I didn't say you could move."

"All right—all right! Take it easy," she soothed. She glanced at the gun, not at all liking how tightly he held it. "Look, Royce, there's a good chance that we're either going to get electrocuted or drown if we stay out here, and you must be hungry and tired. Can't we go somewhere and talk this out? Besides, I'm not sure how long I can keep my hands up like this."

"You'll keep them up for as long as I tell you to." He nodded toward the house. "You want to go in there?"

"We can't. That belongs to my neighbor and—"

"And he isn't here." Lockwood grinned. "That's okay. He's lending it to me while he's gone. Maybe you want to go in there and do something else besides talk?" He watched her turn her eyes away and smirked. "No. I didn't think so. You only like to be touched by Manning, don't you? Well, maybe we'll come back to this interesting subject a little later."

She was instantly alert. "What are you going to do now?"

"I'm going to tie you up, and then we're going to wait for the big man himself to show up." He spoke as though it were the most normal occurrence in the world. "Turn around."

Kendall knew that getting herself tied up was the last thing she could afford to do. Braden had to be out of the shower by now, didn't he? Add a minute or two for him to get dressed and downstairs, and he'd be looking for her. All she needed was to get close enough to the house to warn him...and not get herself shot in the process.

Slowly she turned, careful to keep her legs slightly parted, her knees relaxed. She dropped her gaze to watch the ground for when he came behind her. If only the storm would die down, she thought fleetingly.

"Put your hands behind your head, wrists locked."

Still too far away, she judged. "Royce, this isn't really necessary, you know. We can do this a different way..."

"Do it!" he snapped, poking her in the back with the gun.

Good enough. She bent at the knees, and with all her weight behind her shot her elbow back into his stomach. He doubled over, gasping and coughing. Spinning around, she locked her hands and hammered them onto the back of his neck. He went to his knees, the gun dropping from his hand. Kendall made a grab for it, but he was quick to recover. He grabbed her ankles and sent her flying backward onto the cement edge of Fritz's pen. Pain shot up her right elbow, which took the brunt of her fall. For a moment she was in blind agony. Tears and rain burned into her eyes. She blinked them away in time to see Lockwood picking up her gun. Instinctively she kicked upward, catching the butt with her ankle. More pain followed, but the gun went sailing into the darkness behind the pen.

The fortunate bit of acrobatics temporarily neutralized Lockwood, as well. She'd accidentally caught him in the neck with the edge of her foot, sending him spinning away in a fit of coughing and gagging. It gave Kendall the precious seconds she needed to quell the first wave of nausea her injury had produced.

Her arm was broken; she was sure of it. And it left her with only one option: get away while she could, because she was in no shape to fight Lockwood now. Her gun was as good as lost, and he still had a knife.

She rolled to her left and pushed herself up. Behind her Fritz raced up and down the length of his pen, excited and impatient for his freedom. If she thought he'd be any help at all, she'd free him now, but the probability was that he'd do more harm than good being underfoot.

Lockwood made a blind grab for her, and she ducked it, sending him into Fritz's pen. She didn't stop to see how he'd recovered but took off running as fast as she could. It wasn't fast enough. Lockwood came after her before she'd gone a dozen yards and took her down with a linebacker's tackle. Horrendous pain rose over her in a red tidal wave, and then she felt herself slip into oblivion.

Ten

***

Braden didn't linger long in the shower, but as he was drying off, he noticed how rough his beard was and decided to borrow one of Kendall's disposable razors. He lit the pretty candle she had on the vanity top in order to see, wondering how long the electricity would be off. Maybe it would be a good idea to call it in just in case.

He slipped back into his jeans and shoes, deciding to forgo the shirt. Grabbing his gun, he put out the candle and carefully made his way back downstairs.

The storm was still blowing strong outside, but he noticed that the lightning and thunder had begun to ease a bit. He wondered what Kendall was doing to keep herself occupied. She might like storms, but she was a little leery of lightning.

"Hey, are there any flashlights around this place?" he called, bumping into a side table. "A guy could break his neck around here.... Kendall?"

He groped his way into the kitchen. A flash of lightning temporarily illuminated the room for him, and he saw the open door. Dread convulsed in his stomach and rose, sending a bitter taste into his mouth. He swallowed, raised his gun and stealthily walked toward it.

Holding to the wall, he peered outside as best he could, saw nothing and burst out through the screen door in a crouch. He wheeled around, then rose. She wasn't there. No one was. The temptation to call for her was almost irresistible, but Braden pushed it away. The temptation to go looking for her was equally compelling, but he knew what he had to do first: call for backup.

He charged inside and grabbed the phone. It was dead. Cursing viciously, he jammed it back on the cradle and headed back out.

He hugged the wall and went down the steps, ignoring the rain that drove into his chest and arms like fine needles. He paused at the corner, waiting for that split second of light, and when it came, lunged around it. It was like trying to see through strobe lights in a disco: one second there was utter blackness and the next too much for the eye to behold. He continued cautiously even though every nerve in his body screamed for him to make haste.

His foot bumped into something metallic. He bent and picked it up. It was the meter! Lockwood had cut the seal on the glass housing of the electric meter base and managed to unscrew the band securing the meter to pull it out. He'd even gone so far as to provide himself with insurance by bending the prongs so that it couldn't be replaced into the base.

"Son of a—" Braden flung it away and groped for the wall of the house. If Lockwood was clever enough to pull that stunt, he was probably thorough, as well. Sure enough, a second later Braden's fingers located the telephone lead-in wires and traced them to where they were severed.

"Maybe you blew it there, friend," he said in a deadly whisper. "I just hope to heaven whoever's manning the trace computer tonight is awake and sends out reinforcements."

Kendall! Where's he got you, baby?

Dear God, why did she go out in the first place? And Fritz...where was Fritz? Damn that dog, he'd gotten her to do something crazy again: he was sure of it. And now undoubtedly Lockwood had her. She wouldn't let herself be taken easily, which meant she could be lying somewhere, hurt... He had to find her. Fast. Crouching low, Braden began moving through the darkness like a panther.

He circled the rest of the house, but there were no other signs. Where to look next? The other houses? He looked toward Bruno's, which was barely visible in the driving rain, then toward the Cheeseys' where some of the electrically timed lights Kendall had placed were giving off a mocking, friendly glow. It was closer, so he started in that direction. But the journey proved fruitless. The doors were locked and seemed not to have been tampered with, and when he peered inside the windows, there was no evidence of anyone being there. The tension in him mounted, and his head began to pound. What if Lockwood had her in the sand dunes? Where would he begin to look there?

A forlorn howl broke into the steady rhythm of the rain and echoed Braden's sense of helplessness. He stiffened. *Fritz!* He willed the sound to come again but was rewarded with only the rumble of fading thunder. No matter, he thought. He was fairly certain that the sound had come from the other side of Kendall's house, and that meant Bruno's. He circled down toward the beach and started running.

About two hundred feet from the house he stopped and crouched to scope things out. What he saw made his world turn inside out. Kendall, seemingly unconscious, lay sprawled against a chain link fence with one arm tied high over her head. Behind her in a pen was Fritz, whimpering in concern and nuzzling against her with his nose. Everything in Braden cried out to go to her, but the trap was obvious, and he held back.

He forced himself to move a few dozen yards inland then he checked out the beach. As far as he could tell, everything was clear. Had Lockwood temporarily left her? For how long? And how long did he have once he got in there to release her before he was spotted?

He moved in cautiously. Of course, Fritz spotted him before he was halfway there. The excited yelp he gave echoed in Braden's ears, and he gritted his teeth to repress the urge to yell at the animal to shut up.

When he reached Kendall, he wasn't at all surprised to find that the hand he lifted to her cheek was shaking. Lying there, she looked like someone's abandoned rag doll. Until he felt her pulse, he wasn't even sure that she'd been breathing.

From a distance he'd been confused as to why Lockwood had tied her this way. It had seemed so...casual, but now the reason was all too clear. One glance at the way her right arm lay in her lap, and he knew it was broken. It looked as tragic as a crippled bird's wing, and his heart wrenched in his chest at the thought of how it had happened.

"Kendall...sweetheart...it's me," he whispered gruffly. "Wake up...please. I'm going to untie you." But that was easier said than done. Lockwood had been determined that she stay put, and the knots held stubbornly, especially since Braden was hampered in his movements by the automatic in his right hand.

Kendall moaned softly as she roused from unconsciousness. At first she thought she'd been dreaming that he was here with her, touching her tenderly, anguish in his voice as he spoke. But when she opened her eyes, he was there, and no amount of blinking made him vaporize.

"Oh...no," she moaned, realizing the risk he was taking. "Braden, go. Go away...please! Don't you see? It's a trap."

"Hush," he soothed. "I know. But I'm not going anywhere without you." He concentrated grimly on his task with little success. Frustrated, he glanced over his shoulder. "Where is he—do you know?"

Her lips moved in what might have been a smile or a grimace. "I don't even know how I got here. I passed out, I guess. My arm..."

"I know, love."

"That last tackle was too much for me... the pain was unbearable."

He swore under his breath. Lockwood was going to pay for this one. "Is it still bad?"

"Not when I look at you."

Their gazes locked briefly, and for a split second he felt both immortal and helpless. "Damn! I can't seem to get this... knot... out!"

Impatiently she blinked the rain off her lashes. They hampered her from watching him. He was beautiful like this, a part of the night, a part of the storm. He looked like a fierce warrior with the rain pouring over his body, giving it a glossy sheen, and making his hair almost black.

She shook her head, bemused. Maybe she had a concussion, as well. She was certainly getting...

"Braden! *Behind you!*"

He spinned around like lightning, but Lockwood was already too close. Searing heat scorched across his shoulder blade, momentarily numbing him. His gun wobbled in his right hand, and pouncing on the advantage, Lockwood snatched it from him.

The younger man retreated a few steps, switched the gun into his right hand and tucked away his knife with his left. A look of satisfaction crossed his face as he tested the weight of the gun in his hand. "Now we're ready to start *my* trial," he drawled.

Braden touched his shoulder briefly, glanced at the blood on his fingers and wiped them into his jeans. Then he centered his attention on the smaller man before him. "You're a fool if you think you're going to get away with this."

"Seems to me if anyone's a fool around here, it's you, Manning...and the little lady here." He gave her an amused look. "You want to know something funny? She gave me more of a tussle than you did! She's a scrapper, that one. I respect that," he told her. "That's why I was so nice the way I tied you up. Wasn't that decent of me?"

"Yes. Thank you, Royce."

He laughed. "I like you. You almost take my head off, and then you're polite as hell."

"If you want to be decent to her, let her go," Braden said. "She needs medical attention."

"Relax, Manning. She's tougher than she looks. She gave me this *after* she fell and hurt her arm," he said, indicating his cracked lip. "Anyway, she can't leave now. She's part of this. It wouldn't be complete without her, would it?"

"It's me you've got this gripe with, and we both know it, so what's the point of dragging her into this?" demanded Braden, taking a step toward him.

"Hold it!" warned Lockwood. "I mean it. One more step, and this reunion is all over before it even begins. Now Simon says take one step back and sit." He waited until Braden complied before relaxing his trigger finger. "That's better. The important thing to remember in all this is not to get me nervous. I can't be held responsible for my actions if you get me nervous, so don't go trying to be a big hero to your lady-love here. If you both behave, I might let her go when we're all through. But we're going to do this right. She was here *then* so she has to be here *now*."

"What you're saying is that we're on trial, and you're our judge and jury," Braden jeered. "Why don't you just pull the trigger and get it over with."

"Because that's not the way it's done in the system, is it? In the *system* you're innocent until proven guilty...unless you're a cop, of course, and then no rules apply, and you can shoot anyone you want."

"Whatever they've been feeding you in prison has affected your brain," Braden muttered.

"What's the matter? You get touchy when somebody says it the way it is?"

For a moment Braden looked as if he was about to leap at Lockwood's throat. "Damn your hide—that shot was in self-defense, and you know it!"

"It was murder!"

Kendall's eyes widened in horror as Royce perfected his aim at Braden. "Royce!" she called urgently. She paused, swallowing her fear for Braden. "Don't. Don't lose your temper. Let's talk. Please."

He smirked. "Plea bargaining already?"

"No. That's not what I'm talking about. When I start begging for my life, I'll tell you point-blank."

"Like when you tried to give me karate lessons before?"

She momentarily closed her eyes, fighting off exhaustion and the feeling that it was utterly hopeless to try to deal with him. "Royce, you gave me no choice. You came at me. You interrupted my life...."

"Oh, yeah? Well, let me tell you something, lady. You did more than interrupt mine! The two of you," he amended, waving the gun between them like an accusing finger.

"That's the core of it, isn't it?" she said thoughtfully. "You're angry. And all that anger is swirling around in you like a time bomb. Do you know how much easier your life would be if you talked out some of that anger?"

"Don't play psychiatrist with me."

"When was the last time someone listened to you? Really listened?"

"I don't need anyone to listen to me."

"Of course you do," she said conversationally. "Everyone does. I do. You're only human; don't you get scared sometimes . . . lonely?"

"I've been alone all my life."

"No, you weren't. Not quite. You had Billy."

A nerve ticked in his cheek. "Until you killed him."

"Billy listened to you, didn't he?" she continued ignoring his outburst. "He was a good listener; I remember Braden saying so. He said it showed a bright mind, that Billy was interested in growing. You liked to teach him things, didn't you? And just talk to him because he was special."

"He shouldn't have died. He was a good boy."

"He used to be," she corrected.

He snapped his head around at her and glared. "What are you talking about? He was always a good kid."

"He was once, after Braden started working with him and he got that job after school. Before that he was on his way to being a young hood getting into trouble with street gangs, doing the exact same kind of things that you did at his age. It was like you were his role model. Then Braden started showing him something different, another side of the world, and you didn't like that, did you?"

"That's enough."

"You started to lose control over him then, and it made you jealous. You only had Billy in your life, and if you lost his attention, you thought you'd have nothing, so you started to put ideas in his head, dreams about big money, trying to impress him. It would be easy to get a couple of guns . . . hit a convenience store . . . make some quick money."

"Shut up, will you! You don't know the first thing about the way it was between us."

Kendall licked the rain from her lips and took a steadying breath, aware of how tense Royce was becoming and how quiet and still Braden had grown. "Maybe I do know a little. I know you didn't anticipate things going sour with that holdup. You never intended for Billy to actually have to use that gun you'd gotten for him. But he did...and he died...and the saddest part of all of it is that he got killed trying to free you. And I think you feel bad about that, Royce. You're the one who got him into that mess.

You. But guilt is a terrible thing to carry around, isn't it? It's better to find someone else to blame. Is that how it went with you?''

"Stop it!" he screamed, swinging the gun at her. "I didn't mean for it to happen. I loved him. We were a team. I didn't mean it to happen...." He raised a hand to wipe the tears from his face.

Braden saw his opportunity and leaped for it.

"No!" warned Lockwood.

In one smooth sweep Braden pushed the hand holding the gun up in the air—it discharged—and then he smashed it down onto Royce's knee. Lockwood cried out, the gun fell, and Braden gave him one final blow to the chin, sending him reeling backward. He was probably unconscious before he hit the ground.

Kendall dropped her head back against the fence and closed her eyes. Thank God, she thought. Relief and exhaustion swept over her, leaving her numb. Suddenly it wasn't so bad sitting tied to this fence, in a puddle of water while half the Gulf poured over your head.

She didn't hear Braden come to her, but she felt his hands as soon as they framed her face. She opened her eyes and met his, cherishing and possessive. He kissed her with the most breathtaking gentleness. It brought tears to her eyes.

"I love you," he whispered against her lips. "I love you so much it hurts, and I was terrified wondering if you were going to pull that little stunt off."

"I was terrified that he was going to shoot you," she replied. "I had to do something. Braden, you really did provoke him terribly."

He gave her a sheepish look. "I was disgusted that I'd let him sneak up on me like that."

"I felt the same way."

"You're magnificent. Did you really give him a rough time when he caught you?"

"How do you think I got this?" she demanded, nodding at her useless arm.

His expression changed from admiring to worried. "How does it feel?"

"I'll live. Provided I don't have to spend the rest of my life tied to this fence. I feel like a grounding rod." She tilted her head, trying to see over his shoulder. "How's your back? I saw so much blood..."

"Mostly superficial, I think. Hold on a minute—I'll go get his knife and cut you loose." He rose and started toward Lockwood. Then the sound of an approaching truck had him jogging over to the driveway to flag it down. A moment later Frank pulled up and jumped out of the cab.

He took one sweeping look around and extended his hand to Braden.

"Looks like I timed this one a little too close for comfort," he apologized. He saw Kendall, frowned, and rushed to her side. "Kendall, are you all right?" He touched her cheek affectionately and glanced down at her arm, wincing. "Is it?"

"It is. Ortega, I'd be willing to swap my congratulations cigar for a knife, if you have one."

"What? Oh. Just a second."

"That's what they all say," she muttered. Finally Braden returned with Lockwood's switchblade. When he'd freed her, she rubbed her sore flesh against her cheek. "You want to try to stand, or should I carry you?" he asked her.

"I'd really like to try to stand for a bit."

But she was as wobbly as a newborn colt when he eased her to her feet. "I've got to get you to a hospital," he muttered, encouraging her to let herself lean on him.

"We're both going," she corrected. "But not for a little bit, okay? We can't leave Frank here alone, and neither one of us is in any shape to drive."

Frank joined them after handcuffing Lockwood, who was still out cold. "Want me to go call for some help?"

Braden shook his head. "Our phone is out. Lockwood cut the wires, but that should have signaled somebody downtown, so let's wait a few more minutes and see if anyone shows up." He looked down at Kendall. "Why don't you let me put you in Frank's car for now?"

"How about a walk on the beach?"

"Kendall, you're in no shape for a walk."

"Please? Besides, Fritz will need to run a bit before we lock him up for the night."

Braden glared at the terrier who sat by the pen's gate and observed the proceedings as though he knew what was going on and that he'd come out an eventual winner. "I was planning on letting him finish learning his lesson outdoors tonight.'' Then he remembered that it was the terrier who'd eventually led him to Kendall. ''Oh, all right. Come on out, you oversize wet rat,'' he said, opening the gate.

The terrier took off in a beeline for Kendall's house. ''Well, there's somebody who's more than willing to call it a night,'' Frank said, chuckling.

Kendall smiled. ''Still on cloud nine, new papa?''

''I may never come down,'' he admitted with a self-conscious grin.

''How's Ginger?''

''Tired. I left her sleeping; of course, she did all the work. You can see the baby while you're at the hospital, he added as an enthusiastic afterthought.

Braden bent low to Kendall's ear. ''I think he has this all planned.''

A few minutes later Braden relented and led Kendall down toward the water. The rain had stopped, and the lightning was an occasional flicker in a distant cloud. In the distance a freighter was headed out to sea, its twinkling lights adding magic to a mysterious dark sky. There was a freshness in the air that was also soothing, and Kendall leaned back against Braden's chest and inhaled deeply.

''I always wanted to share this with you,'' she whispered. ''It's so beautiful out here at night. There are so many things to dream about when you look out at that great vastness.''

Braden kissed the top of her head. ''Will you be sorry to leave the water?''

"Oh, no," she said, tilting her head back to look at him. "Anywhere you are will be a place to dream."

His chest rose and fell against her back. "I'll always try to give you plenty to dream about."

She turned her head to kiss the hand on her left shoulder. Then she sighed. "It's going to happen, isn't it?"

"You mean us?"

"Yes."

"You bet it is."

"Poor Royce . . . do you think he'll ever get his life straightened out?"

"He has to want to try."

From behind them came the sound of cars, and they turned to see two police cars pull in. "Looks like the cavalry finally made it," murmured Kendall. She muffled a yawn and leaned her head against Braden. "I think I'm ready to go to the hospital now."

Braden gently picked her up in his arms and kissed her forehead. "Close your eyes and sleep."

Eleven

Braden leaned against the bar and watched the couples on the dance floor sway to the slow romantic tune being played by the three-piece band. Nice party, he thought. It had been three years since he'd attended his last police Christmas party, and though they hadn't changed much, he was glad to be able to admit that he missed them. How his life had changed since that last one.

The bartender approached him. "Can I get you anything, Sarge?"

"Yeah. How about some coffee, Joe?"

The craggy-faced man nodded approvingly and added a rare smile as his glance shifted to the dancers. "You and the missus about to call it a night?"

"If I can ever get her off the dance floor." Braden grinned, took his mug and turned his attention back to the crowd.

He found her easily, unaware of how his expression softened as he did. She'd been shopping for that dress for the better part of a month. It was a teal-colored satin sheath with rhinestone shoulder straps and a slit that made him have second thoughts about letting her wear it. It also had a side zipper that he thought was particularly intriguing. He'd discovered it the night she modeled it for him. Very sexy, he decided then and now.

It was hard to believe that it had already been five months since they'd married. He smiled, remembering how after the Lockwood incident they'd decided not to wait, or waste the rest of their vacation, and had applied for a license the following day. What a sight they'd been, she with her cast and both of them with their arms in a sling. Five months. The days slipped by like minutes. He still found himself reaching for her before he opened his eyes in the morning, unable to convince himself that she was really his. Life was indeed good.

Downing the last gulp of his coffee, Braden set the mug on the bar and went to reclaim his wife. She was dancing with Henry Fielder, who gave him a mock glare when Braden tapped him on the shoulder.

"I don't suppose it would do any good to pull rank?" the captain drawled.

"Marital privileges," Braden replied, with a Cheshire cat smile.

Henry turned back to Kendall and kissed her cheek. "If you ever get tired of this smart aleck, come see me."

She laughed softly. "And what would Alice say to that?"

"Good riddance, probably. It would leave her with more time to dote on the grandkids." He winked at her, patted Braden on the back and left them.

"He's such a darling," murmured Kendall, going into her husband's arms.

"Oh, yeah? Then what does that make me?"

"My darling," she whispered into his ear.

He planted a discreet kiss against her neck and drew her body closer to his. "Mmm...now this feels better. Have I told you how beautiful you look tonight, Mrs. Manning?"

"Several times, Mr. Manning. But don't let that stop you."

"It won't. As popular as you are tonight, I need to make all the points I can. Have I told you that I love you?"

She nodded solemnly. "Once this morning, twice when you got home this afternoon, and every time we've danced this evening."

"Just checking." He smiled down into her twinkling eyes."

"Having a good time?"

"A lovely time, but I saw you drinking coffee. Are we getting ready to leave?"

He raised the hand he held to his lips. "Would you be disappointed? I have a sudden craving to be alone with my wife...maybe snuggle on the couch and watch the lights on the Christmas tree...sip hot chocolate...lick marshmallow off your lips..."

"Last one to the car has to get up and put the coffee on in the morning."

In a short while they'd said their goodbyes and were on their way home.

The house they now lived in was one they bought two months after their wedding. Braden's apartment had proved to be too small and depressing. Once Kendall had convinced him to come out and look at the immaculate little house she'd discovered, with the sun room in the back and the big oak trees, he'd been unable to refuse her plea to use her savings as a down payment.

As he drove into their driveway now, his feeling of contentment deepened. He noted the gaily ribboned wreath illuminated by the entry light. It was just another of Kendall's touches that made it home. Home... Despite her demanding job working with welfare kids for a social service bureau, she'd managed to create just that. It was a warm, inviting environment for the two of them that he eagerly returned to each night, no matter what kind of day he'd had.

Kendall's thoughts weren't dissimilar to Braden's. She, too, was glad to be home. The party had been even more fun than she'd anticipated; it was good to see her former co-workers and catch up with what was going on in their lives. Tomorrow Braden's parents were due to arrive, and they would stay through Christmas. As excited as she was about having them,

Kendall was even more eager to have this time alone with Braden.

"I'll make the hot chocolate; why don't you turn on the tree lights?" she said, once they were inside and had removed their coats. "The mail is on the coffee table. I didn't have time to get to it earlier. Why don't you browse through it?"

"I'll wait for you." They'd probably be mostly Christmas cards, and he got more pleasure out of watching her open them. She pored over each one like a child receiving a surprise gift. Before she could go off to the kitchen, he grabbed her and kissed her breathless.

"Mmm . . . what was that for?"

"Incentive to hurry."

Kendall's smile was mischievous as she set out the mugs and waited for the milk to heat. Everything was going perfectly. She had been planning this evening, this moment, for days . . . even down to the piece of mail tucked between the rest. It was just as well that he wanted to wait for her, because she so wanted to see the expression on his face.

When she returned to the living room, he had a tape playing romantic music on the stereo and was stretched out on the couch. He'd removed his jacket and vest, tie and shoes, and his hands were clasped behind his head.

"You look comfy," she said, setting the tray on the coffee table. She slipped out of her shoes and sighed. "I've been wanting to do that for the past hour."

Braden sat up, shifted his feet to the floor and drew her down beside him. "I've noticed you've been wearing lower heels lately. Don't tell me that you've finally met your match in those kids of yours?"

"There's one or two that might get me to yet, but it's not that." She smiled as he swung her legs onto his lap. "Lower heels are just healthier, that's all."

"If you say so. Anyway, I thought your feet looked very sexy tonight."

"So speaks the man with the foot fetish."

"Darling, all your parts are a fetish with me."

She handed him his mug, topped with a generous dollop of marshmallow cream, then reached for her own. "Ah...heaven."

"The perfect ending to a perfect day." With his free hand he began to massage her feet. They fascinated him; they were so small and delicately shaped, and though she rarely wore nail polish on her hands, she always had some sexy color on her toes.

"Absolutely." She murmured softly under his gentle ministration. "Do that for five minutes, and I'll be ready for a total replay."

"Would you settle for foreplay?" he asked, nipping the graceful arch of one foot.

"Oh, I could be coerced into changing my mind. Braden—that tickles!" Her giggle turned into a gasp as her hot chocolate sloshed precariously in the mug. Braden released her, but only to lift her completely onto his lap.

"Come here where you belong."

She tried unsuccessfully to drag the hem of her dress back down over her thighs. "I can see that I'm not going to get another wearing out of this dress before it goes to the cleaners."

"If you keep wiggling around like that, I won't guarantee I'll leave enough of it in one piece to bother taking it there." His palm slid along her smooth thigh in a sensuous prowl and disappeared beneath her dress. "You have marshmallow on your lip. Don't move." As he took great care in removing it for her with his lips and tongue, the slow exploration of his hand finally settled on stroking the heart of her warmth with equal care.

She moaned softly. "I'm going to drop this stuff all over us in a second."

"Glad to see that the honeymoon isn't over."

"You're insatiable."

"So are you."

"So handsome and so swollen-headed." She kissed him on the cheek chastely. "Aren't we going to open the mail?"

"I can't really say it's foremost on my mind. Okay." He shrugged at the look she gave him. "But you're only prolonging the inevitable."

"It titillates the imagination."

"'Titillates?'" he mouthed.

"You'll see." She set down her mug and reached for the stack. There was a card from Bruno, and the Cheeseys sent another postcard from their latest expedition. "They're going skiing next," murmured Kendall, reading the back.

"Glad to see they're taking things slower since Fred slipped his disk diving into the Mediterranean last summer," drawled Braden.

"Where do you suppose they'll go?"

"The Alps."

"But they can't ski! Surely it'll be someplace like Colorado or New Mexico."

"Can't?" he guffawed. "You're talking about the Lewis and Clark of Corpus Christi. Bet you another romantic Manning dinner that I'm right," he challenged, the gleam in his eye reminding her of the last one they'd shared.

She'd come home one evening, exceptionally tired and depressed from one of her cases, only to be met at the door by him wearing a bath towel and a smile. He'd led her to the bathroom, where a steaming bubble bath waited, with candles everywhere and a TV tray holding a pizza and a bottle of wine set beside the tub.

Kendall wet her lips. "You're on. But how do I top yours if I lose?"

"If you lose, forget the main course and concentrate on the appetizer and dessert like you did last time."

Kendall didn't think that he could say or do anything to make her blush anymore, but he'd just proved her wrong. Clearing her throat, she reached for the next card. It was from Frank and Ginger, and they'd sent a family picture. "Michelle's going to have her mother's hair and her father's dark eyes," she murmured. "Oh, and they want us to come down for a weekend after the holidays."

"Great."

There were close to a dozen cards in all. She found her father's most touching, and Adam's, as usual, the most witty.

She picked up the last envelope, a small frown puckering her brow. "Hmm...what's this? A typed envelope addressed to Mr. Braden Manning, sans Mrs., with no return address."

Braden took a long sip of his drink. "Maybe I should take it to forensics and have them fingerprint it."

"Or maybe I should sniff-test it and see if it's an old girlfriend trying to be semidiscreet."

"I never had any discreet girlfriends, semi or otherwise," he teased. "Go on, open it."

"Not after that crack, bud. It's all yours."

Still chuckling, Braden set down his drink and took the envelope, ripping it open without his wife's usual care. He pulled out the card, his smile growing puzzled as he noticed the childish motif. When he read the words *To Daddy* written across the top, he looked positively flabbergasted. "What in the..."

He yanked it open, his eyes racing to the bottom where a childish scrawl read:

Merry Christmas, Daddy.
See you in July!
LOVE,
BABY MANNING I

Braden read it again in disbelief. When he looked up at Kendall, he found her watching him, anxiously nibbling on her lower lip.

"You wrote this."

"Well, it's a little early yet for him, or her, to hold a pen."

"You... you're..." He swallowed with difficulty. "A baby?" he whispered thickly.

Slowly she nodded, the expression on his face causing tears to flood her eyes.

"A baby... we're... you..." He gave up trying to say anything intelligible and crushed her into his arms, rocking and laughing and bestowing bewildered, joyous kisses all over her tearstained face.

"So you're pleased?" she sniffed.

"*Pleased?* I'm...I'm thrilled...ecstatic...I'm...I can't even get the blasted words to come out." He cupped her face between his hands and kissed her until she was clinging to him. "I love you, Kendall Manning." He touched her still-flat tummy and closed his eyes, but his wet lashes were evidence enough of how deeply moved he was. He drew a long ragged breath. "I can't believe anything could make me happier than I was at the moment I finally got my ring on your finger, but you've managed it."

"What a lovely thing to say."

"July... you're two months along?"

She nodded.

"And you've seen a doctor? Who is he or she?"

"No one I think you'd know."

"But they're reliable?" he persisted, missing the laughter in her eyes. "You're okay? When do they want us to sign up for those breathing classes? I wonder if Frank still has any of those books . . ."

She sat back and allowed him to ramble, content to watch him spin dreams all night if he wanted. What a Christmas this was going to be, and what a special gift they were going to be able to give his parents. From the moment he'd introduced her to them, they'd made no secret of the fact that it would be more than all right to make them grandparents.

"Kendall."

Braden's husky whisper brought her out of her own daydreaming, and their eyes locked. His hands hadn't stopped moving over her since he'd discovered her news, but now they were slowing into a sensual rhythm that echoed the desire shimmering in his eyes. He moved his mouth along her jaw, down her neck, along her collarbone. "I want you. Now. I want to make love with you."

She could feel the urgency rising in his body and transmitting its need to hers. It wasn't unlike that night months ago when they'd made love on her couch, only this time there wasn't the shadow of danger haunting them.

"Here?"

"No, not here," he said, sweeping her up into his arms and heading for their bedroom. "Tonight I want the comfort and space to do a thorough job."

She wrapped her arms around his neck. "You've always done a thorough job," she replied impishly.

"Oh, tiger . . . you haven't seen anything yet."

*   *   *   *   *

Silhouette Desire

COMING NEXT MONTH

#373 INTRUSIVE MAN—Lass Small
How could Hannah Calhoun continue to run her boardinghouse with any
semblance of sanity when all her paying guests were pushing her into the
all-too-willing arms of Officer Maxwell Simmons?

#374 HEART'S DELIGHT—Ashley Summers
Cabe McLain was resigned to a life of single parenthood—but that was
before Laura Richards showed him that her childhood friendship had
ripened into a woman's love.

#375 A GIFT OF LOVE—Sherryl Woods
Meg Blake had learned early on that most problems were best dealt with
alone. Matt Flanagan was the one to show her otherwise—teaching her
firsthand the power of love.

#376 SOMETHING IN COMMON—Leslie Davis Guccione
Confirmed bachelor Kevin Branigan, the "cranberry baron" from
STILL WATERS (Desire #353), met Erin O'Connor—and more than
met his match!

#377 MEET ME AT MIDNIGHT—Christine Flynn
Security agent Matt Killian did things by-the-book. He had no intention
of having an unpredictable—and all too attractive—Eden Michaels on his
team. But soon Matt found himself throwing caution to the winds.

#378 THE PRIMROSE PATH—Joyce Thies
It took an outrageous scheme from their respective grandparents to
find the adventurous hearts beneath banker Clay Chancelor's and
CPA Carla Valentine's staid exteriors. Neither imagined that the prize at
the end of the chase was love.

AVAILABLE NOW: